IRREVOCABLY DAMNED

To my Family,
Mom, Dad, Dani,
& Peteys!

Thank you for all
of your
love and
Support!

Love always,
Jessica S.

IRREVOCABLY DAMNED

Jessica S. Leigh

iUniverse, Inc.
New York Bloomington Shanghai

Irrevocably Damned

iUniverse books may be ordered through booksellers or by contacting:

iUniverse
1663 Liberty Drive
Bloomington, IN 47403
www.iuniverse.com
1-800-Authors (1-800-288-4677)

Because of the dynamic nature of the Internet, any Web addresses or links contained in this book may have changed since publication and may no longer be valid.

This is a work of fiction. All of the characters, names, incidents, organizations, and dialogue in this novel are either the products of the author's imagination or are used fictitiously.

ISBN: 978-0-595-50781-8 (pbk)
ISBN: 978-0-595-61646-6 (ebk)

Printed in the United States of America

Thanks to my mom, dad, and sister.
I could never have done this without you.

Preface

She looked to the shadows in horror as a low, mellow voice called out to her. "It's nice of you to join me, Serene." She couldn't quite make out the face of the man speaking to her. His figure moved smoothly in the shadows of the trees. Blood was steadily seeping from the cuts and scrapes peppering her body as she looked around hurriedly.

Fear crept through her as she came to the realization that she was alone in this. No one was coming to help her—no one. She was going to have to face this alone. But she was ready. Damian had prepared her for this.

Then why was it that as she stood there she found herself shaking; her breathing coming out in deep, raspy puffs.

Serene's mind was racing as she followed his silhouette with her piercing green eyes, never glancing away from the man she knew she had to kill. Everything was weighing on her. It was either his death or her own. Never in a million years would Serene have pictured herself in this situation, about to battle to the death with a man she didn't know. All she knew was that he wanted her dead for reasons she may never understand.

Her hands dropped to her side, searching for the dagger she had been equipped with and her stomach lurched in horror as her hand brushed her flat jeans. Her weapon was gone. Her palms were empty. The herbal remedy was gone as well. In her haste to find salvation she had dropped them in the woods, too rushed to remember to pick them up. She was unarmed and helpless.

Serene soon became aware of the eerie silence slinking across the woods. The only sound audible to her ears was that of her raspy breathing. Suddenly, as if grasping her thoughts, the shadow spoke again.

"I'm sorry that it has to be this way, but you've left me no choice." The man began to advance from the shadows and his face was slowly illuminated by the soft glow of the moon overhead. A chilling, sickening fear spread out through Serene's body as her eyes locked with his. How could this be happening? No, this was impossible. It couldn't be. As he advanced closer to her, she stumbled back, her knees shaking horribly.

CHAPTER 1

"None of this makes sense," she muttered under her breath, eyes swimming with the words that sprawled across the pages before her. A glance to the clock broke her disinterested concentration. A bit longer. The pages of her books zoomed in and out of focus as she drifted from daydream to reality and back again. Chemistry had never been a strong point in Serene's life. Would she ever really need to know the number of protons in Iron? And when was she actually going to be faced with the decision of which chemicals to mix without burning down the house? Chemistry was like Wood Shop to Serene. Interesting at a glance, but full of skills she'd never actually need. Her thought process was broken and she looked back at the clock as her mind began to spin. 'Five, four, three, two, one,' she thought as she counted down in her head.

"Serene, dinner," came a voice from downstairs.

"Right on schedule," Serene muttered to herself as she did most nights. Every night for the past eleven years, Silvia Valance had prepared dinner and had it set out on the table squarely at six-sixteen. Serene, no matter how long she pondered, could never figure out why her mother acted this way or why it was always at such a peculiar time. Her mother had always been punctual and would probably prove to be so for many years to come, so Serene would always count on having dinner at six-sixteen.

She descended the carpeted stairs, into the living room where the aroma of hickory ham and green beans lingered in the air. Pictures from past years hung in an orderly fashion on the cream colored walls. Serene paused at one of she and her father from when she was quite young. A portrait of she and mother followed. Both Serene and Silvia wore matching dresses, her mother's idea, and were positioned in front of a fake snow scene. Christmas portraits were a yearly to-do for the Valance family. Following was a line of school pictures from first grade up to her current eleventh grade photo, each equally as horrid as the next in Serene's mind, though the past few years without braces helped drastically.

Walking into the dinning room, Serene smiled at her mother who was sporting her newest red dress. Silvia, having been raised by rather strict parents, found it proper to dress up for dinner. While most families only dress up for special occasions such as Thanksgiving or Christmas, Silvia made a point of wearing her best, not once in a while, but rather every single night of the week. She also found it necessary to have a disc of opera music playing ever so faintly in the background. As the years passed Serene had grown use to her mother's odd rituals and found that they were now practically unnoticeable, though Serene had yet to develop a taste for opera.

The dinning room was classy. A crystal chandelier hung above the table and a white candle burned as the center piece. The table could seat eight, but it would just be Serene and her mother, just as it had been since Serene's father left. Several moments passed before Serene looked to her mother pensively. "I really hope that dad keeps his promise about spending the summer with him in England. I haven't even seen him since I was like five. Hopefully this time won't be like all the others," she said before finishing off her biscuit which she had been eagerly munching on between sentences.

"You mustn't be too hard on your father, Serene. He's a very busy man, running his own business and all. You must understand that." Silvia watched her daughter while removing her napkin from her lap and placing it on the table.

"Yeah, but be realistic. Sure, he's busy, but 'not seeing your daughter for more than twelve years' busy? He could at least write more often. I doubt he even remembers what I look like." Serene's gaze drifted to her plate as she picked at her beans with her fork.

"Serene, you know your father loves you. Why else would he be willing to have you stay with him for the entire summer? Luther may have made some mistakes in his life, but he's not a bad man. I wouldn't have married him if I didn't have trust in him. But try not to be upset if the plans fall through. Things come up at a moments notice for a man like your father. Be patient with him. He'll come around," Silvia said as she kept her eyes on her daughter.

"A bit late for that, don't you think?" she questioned in a rather cynical tone. Serene had been subject to enough of her fathers 'mistakes'. She was sick and tired of getting her hopes up only to have them crushed time and time again. As she sat there, picking at her food, she drifted into thoughts of how wonderful her summer would be if her father actually kept his promise this time around.

Serene had always dreamed of visiting England. Living in the same town for seventeen years, she sometimes forgot that there was an entire world to explore. Only time would tell if this summer would turn out that way she prayed and hoped it would. She glanced down to her plate, which was now nearly empty, only scraps of food here and there. Standing, she carried her plate and half empty glass with her, carting it off to the kitchen. Silvia followed and the two of them cleaned the plates in silence.

Just as the night sky began to grow steadily darker, Serene and her mother finished cleaning the dishes.

"I guess I'm gonna go to bed. Night." Serene kissed her mother on the cheek and left the kitchen.

As she reached her room she pushed the door open gently, entered, and closed it softly behind her. She pounced on her bed, sighing deeply as she turned over on her back. Grasping her phone off her bedside table, she punched several digits quickly, without error, as if she had dialed it repeatedly. Placing the phone to her ear, a smile twitched on her lips. A soft, deep voice answered on the other end.

"Hello?"

"Hey Ben," she cooed, flipping onto her stomach, her once small smile, now a broad grin.

"Hey babe," rang Ben's voice over the telephone. Ben Carden and Serene had been a couple for more than two years. In fact, their three-year anniversary was merely two days off. Serene had never been so happy or excited in her life. She loved Ben with such a passion that words, nor actions could adequately attest. Whenever she saw him she felt butterflies in her stomach. She loved him with all her heart and soul and nothing would ever separate them. And while her passion for him grew every day that they were together, there was still something missing in their relationship and, for whatever reason, Serene could not figure it out.

"What have you been up to? Running off on some secret affair?" he joked, giving a deep laugh.

Serene giggled a bit, smiling. "Damn, you've caught me," she joked back. "Two days until our three-year anniversary. Dinner? Movie?" She was determined to pry whatever he had planned out of him.

"Dinner and a movie? What kind of a boyfriend do you think I am? Unoriginal? No, I have something else planned." There was a slight underlying tone of mystery to his voice. Serene grinned, fantasizing all of the fantastic things he could have planned. She bit her lip lightly, growing anxious. She stood, pulling the phone cord along behind her as she paced to her closet. Pushing the doors open, she began to flick through her clothing.

"So Benjamin," she teased, "what type of attire shall I wear to this fabulous event?" She held several tops up against her body, viewing her reflection in her mirror.

"Everything looks fine on you, so whatever you want."

"I'm sorry that I have to leave to go with my dad on the same day as our anniversary."

"It's alright. At least it's not until later at night," replied Ben.

"True."

Serene hung a sleek red top on the hook on the back of her closet door. She returned to her bed, sitting with one leg hanging off the side and one leg tucked under her. "Alright, well, I'm going to bed so I'll talk to you tomorrow."

She smiled weakly as she and Ben finished their goodbyes and hung up. A simple good-bye and that was it, no 'I love you'. Nothing. Serene feared the 'L' word as if was the plague. Only bad things could come from such a commitment. Ben had attempted several times to declare his love for her, but she had stopped him in his tracks, nearly breaking his heart in the process. It hurt her to hurt him, but as hard as she tried her fear controlled her and kept her from sharing her love for him.

The night soon came to an end and Serene, crawling into bed around ten-thirty, drifted into fantastic dreams of the life that she and Ben would someday share. It was an improbable high school romance and no matter how many times she was told that no one ever marries their high school sweet heart, she never listened. Serene knew, deep in her heart, that she was destined to love Ben and only Ben. Loving another would be a sin in her eyes and she couldn't live without him. When she was with Ben she could escape from her past. She could forget that her parents were divorced. She could forget how unreliable her father was. She could simply forget and escape with him. But now, as she laid curled up under her covers, she was forced to remember.

Serene's parents, Silvia and Luther, had divorced when she was just five years old. Luther had moved off to England to begin his own business, selling exquisite gems to the richest people that walked the Earth. Every summer since Serene was seven her father had sworn that he would take the summer off to come and visit her, rescuing her from the dull town of Covington, Virginia. For ten years straight he had shattered his promise, leaving Serene with a broken heart. He always had some excuse. As Serene grew older she learned that his excuses were simply that, excuses. According to Silvia, the truth of the matter was that Serene's father had always battled an addiction to gambling. Not crack or cocaine, but perhaps worse. He was a con man, constantly evading bookies who he owed thousands if not millions of dollars to, which was why he couldn't take a second to visit Serene.

She faintly recalled a time in her life when her father had lived with her and her mother. She remembered him coming home incredibly late most evenings, and sometimes not at all. As Serene turned four her mother and father argued constantly. The neighborhood began to talk and the Valance family became a topic of gossip. Luther complained that Silvia nagged him too much and Silvia argued that Luther was lazy and that he never got up on time or came home at night. And both were correct. The two were married for six years before they divorced. Serene never really figured out why her parents had split up or what caused them to fight so much. They told her they just weren't meant to be, but she figured there was something more to it. All she knew was that things were better now. She would be a senior next year and there were only three more days of school left before summer with her dad. As the moon filled the night sky, Serene drifted to sleep, sweet thoughts of summer lingering in her mind.

Serene awoke early the next morning, slamming her hand on the alarm clock humming loudly in her ear. She drug herself to the bathroom and turned on the shower, running her hand under the water every now and then to test the temperature. When she was pleased she disrobed and jumped hurriedly into the shower, shivering for a moment as the stiff air in the room made contact with her body. As she stood in the shower, the water dripping from her hair, she smiled to herself, thinking of how lucky she was. She was three days away from the best summer vacation of her life, she was madly in love with the boy of her dreams, and to top it all off, she was spending the night at her friend Hailey's house.

After fifteen minutes in the shower, Serene stepped out, turning the water off, and wrapped a towel snugly around her, shivering once more at the moment of chill. She stood at the mirror, examining her once straight, but now wet, curled hair. Her chocolate brown hair, which had been perfectly straight the night before, had now returned to its original state, curly. She scoffed at her reflection in the mirror. Oh how she disliked her curled hair sometimes. This was the exact reason she spent an hour a night straightening it. Today, however, she had decided against wasting an hour of her life to her hair. While she didn't mind her curls that much, everyone else seemed to like it much better straightened. She flicked on the blow dryer and spent ten more minutes in the bathroom drying her chestnut locks, allowing them to fall gently around her face. What a hassle it was being a girl. She then spent another ten minutes applying her make-up. Eyeliner, eye shadow, blush, and of course lip gloss. She breathed a sigh of relief as she departed from the bathroom and got dressed, sliding into a skirt and a red v-neck top.

Silvia Valance was rushing around frantically just a floor below Serene, putting together last minute presentations for her job. Serene appeared at the foot of the stairs a moment later, books in hand and ready to go. She leaned against the wall, waiting for her mother.

"Serene? Have you seen my note cards and glasses?" her mother yelled from the kitchen in a rather exasperated voice.

Serene didn't even bother answering and she didn't need to.

"Oh, never mind I've found them." Silvia burst through the kitchen door a second later, rushing to the front door, scooping up her keys and adjusting the glasses that were resting atop her head. "Off we go then." She tossed the door open and ushered Serene out as she closed the door behind her. Silvia dropped Serene off at school and than sped off, ranting about being late.

Two girls came bursting from the school doors, smiling and giggling as usual.

Hailey Shore and Marissa Banks had been Serene's best friends ever since they were in elementary school. They were practically never apart. They always traveled together, ate together, shopped together. Everything. Of course, they argued every now and then, but what friends didn't? Serene was immediately bombarded with hugs.

"Big day tomorrow! You and Ben will have been going out for three years and you leave for England," Hailey cooed, smiling broadly. She was quickly backed up by Marissa and the two girls began to converse over how they wished they had a boyfriend like Ben and how lucky Serene was to be spending the summer away from Covington. The three of them walked to their first class together as the bell chimed throughout the school. Serene took a deep breath, preparing herself for the day ahead of her. Long, boring, and no doubt filled with unwanted drama and gossip.

The day had been uneventful, though the air at school was charged with the excitement that came with the last few days of class. She, Hailey, and Marissa chatted all the way home about the latest rumors which were now hurriedly traveling through the school, whether by mouth or text message. The ten minute walk home seemed like ages after suffering through such a long day. Serene and Marissa walked Hailey to her house before heading off to theirs'.

"See you tonight at Hailey's," Marissa said as she headed up her front porch.

The five minute walk from Marissa's to her own house gave Serene time to think in peace. The excitement of summer with her father was building in Serene, but new thoughts were beginning to dampen her enthusiasm. She was leaving, flying across the ocean, and Ben was staying in Covington for the summer. Could their relationship survive three months apart? In reality, three months isn't that long, but to a teen girl and her boyfriend it's practically a year. Would Ben fall in love with someone else?

Would Serene find a summer romance in England?

Suddenly, leaving seemed like a bad idea.

Serene pushed all thought from her mind as she reached her house.

Placing her books down on the table beside the front door she noticed 'New Message' blinking on the answering machine. She hit 'Play' and Ben's voice boomed out from the speaker.

"Can't wait for tomorrow babe. Call me later."

She smiled slightly before turning and heading off to her room. She immediately set to work, shoving pajamas and fresh clothing into a bag as well as her toothbrush, hair comb, and perfume. She slung the bag over her shoulder and headed back downstairs. Dropping her bag by the door, she headed off to the living room where she collapsed onto the couch and flicked on the television. After spending ten minutes flipping through the channels and finding nothing that caught her attention, she turned off the TV, sighing out of boredom. Silvia hurried through the front door not too much later and went straight to her room, preparing to take a shower.

Half an hour later, Serene was ready to go to Hailey's house. She left a note on the dinning room table, telling her mother that she had left, and walked down the hall and out the front door.

Hailey sat in her living room, counting the minutes until her friends were to arrive. It was a very rare occasion that Hailey would have a sleepover. Her parents, much like Serene's mother, were very strict. The fear of their white carpets being ruined by a dropped chip was enough to make their heads spin.

The doorbell rang and Hailey sprang to her feet. "I'll get it!"

Wrenching the door open, she revealed Serene with a quaint smile on her face. "Serene! Finally! Come on in." She pulled the door open further, allowing Serene to enter. "Marissa's not here yet," she stated, attempting to close the door, but found it resisting her efforts.

"Your closing the door on my face, Hailey," came a slightly annoyed voice from just behind the door. Hailey blushed a deep maroon and opened the door. A red nosed Marissa was standing on the door step, bags in one hand, the other caressing her face. She slid into the house and closed the door behind her. "Well," she chirped, glancing to Serene and Hailey, "why are we just standing around? Let's get this party started!" And so it began.

The night was filled with makeovers, prank phone calls, dancing, chatting, eating, and movies. It was one in the morning before the girls began to settle down for the night.

"So Serene, what are you and Ben doing tomorrow? Dinner and the movies?" whispered Hailey, making sure not to wake her parents who were all the way down the hall but Hailey feared had supersonic hearing.

"No. That's what I thought too, but he says that he has something better planned." She closed her eyes, relaxing and wondering what he could possibly mean. She waited a moment, expecting Marissa to join in, but the only sound that escaped her was a low grunt of a snore. Apparently she had already drifted into a deep sleep. "Well, we'll see I suppose. Goodnight," whispered Serene.

"Goodnight." Hailey rolled over, drifting into sleep as well. Serene remained awake a while longer, pondering what Ben could possibly have planned for tomorrow. She drifted in and out of dreams.

Dreams about Ben, about her dad, about the summer that was awaiting her. Her life seemed to finally be shaping up. Everything appeared to be perfect.

As she rested her eyes she blinked every now and then, allowing the stray beams of moonlight filtering in through the window to shine brilliantly on her eyes. Looking out the window, she watched the stars, wondering what they had in store for her.

Was her destiny with Ben? The course of her life was busy in the works, preparing to reveal itself when she least expected it. Time was slowly slipping away and, although she was unaware of it, her future was arriving at a rapid pace. As her eyes began to droop shut, her mind swam through blissful dreams of what she wished was to come. Sadly, dreams are merely dreams and fate was about to step in leaving Serene with her dreams, and only her dreams, as a source of escape.

Serene awoke early the next morning, her friends still snoring around her. She stood and carefully stepped over them as she walked to the window. Glancing out, her eyes scanned the skies which were strewn with several white clouds, but other than that the weather was lovely. Her stomach gave a lurch as she remembered that today was her anniversary. She smiled to herself and walked out of the room, heading down the hall to the bathroom. The bathroom tiles were cold against her bare feet and she shivered a bit as she glanced to the mirror, pulling her hair up into a loose bun with strands hanging out here and there. She stumbled from the bathroom and back to Hailey's room.

Her friends were awake and already chatting up a storm. For as long as Serene could remember she had always been slightly different from her friends. Hailey and Marissa were the type of girls who adored shopping, going tanning and, most of all, gossiping. They were ones to flirt with every Tom, Joe, and Harry they met on the street. Serene, on the other hand, enjoyed simpler things. She dreamed to fall in love and be swept away. She found that she'd rather spend an entire day sitting in a field looking up at the sky than store hopping in the mall. And then there was Ben. Ben made her feel complete. He was her knight in shining armor and her savior. She could never imagine being without him.

Several minutes passed and stomachs began to growl. They retreated downstairs for a large breakfast of pancakes, bacon and eggs. The smell alone would make anyone's mouth water.

"So Serene, are you excited about your date with Ben tonight?" Serene wasn't given a second to answer before Marissa continued on. "I know I would be. Just remember, protection is the way to go." Marissa's words went in one ear and right out the other.

Serene had heard the same comment numerous times from Marissa. She and Ben hadn't even gone as far as a heavy make-out session. She opened her mouth to speak, but Marissa continued on.

"And make sure you tell him you love him tonight! I mean, you two have been dating for ages now and you still haven't said it. He might start to lose interest. I could have sworn I saw him eyeing Heather from my math class the other day." Marissa picked at her food disdainfully, the thought of consuming so many calories causing her to think twice. A bite of eggs or two later she looked to Serene who had not responded to her rants. "Sorry. Forget I said anything."

And so Serene did.

Brushing off her friend's rampage she ate her meal quietly with a pensive expression. After she cleared her plate, she helped Marissa with the dishes and retreated upstairs to get her bag.

Waiting by the door for the arrival of her mother, thoughts of the night ahead were swirling through her abstract mind. Even at the age of seventeen she felt that she held the wisdom of the world. She knew what it felt like to be in love. The butterflies that hovered in her stomach when she neared Ben, the dreams at night that she shared with no one but herself, and the smile that never faded from her soft pink lips at the thought of him. It was a feeling that comes perhaps once or twice in a lifetime. Serene thought she had seen everything there was to see and experienced everything there was to experience.

She was wrong.

A black Mercedes pulled up out front, emitting a curt honk. Serene recognized it as her mother and emerged from the house, her bag swinging gracefully by her side. Sliding into the passenger seat she shot her mother a smile, yet her mind wandered elsewhere. As the car pulled away Serene stared, transfixed on the white dashes that lined the road. Her watching, yet unseeing eyes, flashed with thoughts as if in a dream like state. In a mere six hours she would be rushing into Ben's arms. The thought caused a smile to flash broadly across her face. Her mother was too preoccupied fumbling with the radio and paying attention to the road to give much notice to her daughter, but this hardly fazed Serene. She had other things to keep her mind thoroughly preoccupied.

Ben ... Ben ... and more Ben.

CHAPTER 2

Night began to fall on the small town and Serene stood in front of her vanity mirror, examining her reflection with a critical eye. She straightened her top and smoothed out her skirt. Tousling her hair a bit, she gave a sexy pout, her reflection pouting back at her. She looked amazing to say the least.

Perfect.

A small spurt of perfume added the finishing touches, leaving a warm vanilla scent lingering on her smooth, tan flesh. Waltzing to her bed, a violent vibration emitted from her bedside table. Glancing down she spotted her cell phone shaking madly, Bens name flashing across the screen. A smile played across her features and she picked up the phone, flipping it open and pressing it firmly against her ear.

"Hello?"

"I'm outside babe," came Ben's voice from the ear piece on the phone.

Serene laughed a bit and responded before hanging up. She grabbed her purse, slung it over her shoulder, and headed downstairs. Her mother caught her just as she was opening the door.

Silvia went into a long, tedious speech about well behaved young ladies, the outcome of drugs, rape and even something about the dangers of roller coasters which seemed completely irrelevant to the conversation in its entirety. Serene rolled her eyes, but knew that her mother was simply looking out for her. A kiss goodnight and she was out the door, beaming at Ben as she opened the passenger side door and slid in. She was immediately pulled into a kiss, tender and gentle. She pulled back slowly, biting her lip as she ran a hand through his hair. She laughed and her eyes flashed with joy as she pulled her seat belt across her chest, fastening it with a sharp 'Click'.

Speeding off down the street, a smug yet charming smirk forming on his lips, Ben glanced over momentarily, his eyes fixating on Serene.

"You look beautiful," he said, his eyes beaming with happiness.

Tearing his gaze from the goddess sitting next to him, he glanced back to the road, turning left down one street and right a moment later. It was a maze of black asphalt, twisting and winding ahead of them as if trying to tempt them into making a wrong move.

Serene, excitement growing within her, watched the road, trying to map out exactly where they were going. Try as she may, she was left dumbfounded after at least fifteen minutes of driving through the darkened roads.

"Ben, where are you taking me?" she asked with a twinge of impatience. Impatience. A trait she picked up from her father's side no doubt.

"That's for me to know, and you to find out." Ben smiled, keeping his eyes trained on the road.

He often gave such mysterious answers. That was some-thing Serene loved about him. He could turn even the sim-plest surprise into an amazing adventure. Leaning back in her seat, she sighed slightly. Not from frustration or anger, but more so from being overwhelmed with excitement. The stars above shown down with a twinkle that might suggest they knew something no one else did. Serene watched them glow-ing, her eyes in a fixed trance on them for sometime before she snapped out of it, her mind zooming back to reality.

The car had stopped and when Serene looked to Ben, she found that he was no longer beside her.

A warm breeze brushed against Serene's cheek and when she looked over in the direction it had come from she found Ben, holding the car door open for her and smiling a suave, charming smile, his eyes magnificent and green in the moon-light. A smile spread across her rosy lips and, grasping his hand as he extended it, she stepped from the car.

Taking her first good look at where they were, she smiled. No. She didn't simply smile. She positively beamed. The scen-ery was amazing. The car was parked atop a cliff, overlooking the town which looked like a miniature display, lights gleam-ing in all directions. The moon shone high above them, pro-viding an eerie gleam of white light, showering the ground with its rays and the stars sparkled on, dancing for all the world even if no one cared to watch. The grass beneath her feet was the perfect shade of green, each blade cut to perfec-tion. A single willow tree swooped to the ground not too far off, and a black blanket laid sprawled out on the ground to the left of it.

"Ben, it's—amazing." Words couldn't capture the moment in its entirety. Serene, and only Serene, would ever truly grasp how she felt at the moment.

"I hoped you would like it," came Ben's voice in a soft whisper as he walked up from behind her, setting his hands on her hips and kissing the top of her head. Looking out over the cliff and the view beyond, he smiled to himself, realizing that he was the luckiest guy alive. He was madly in love with the most beautiful girl he had ever met and it was their three-year anniversary. They were together at a location so heavenly that words could not describe it, and nothing was going to ruin the perfect night he had planned out.

"I love it Ben," she responded, turning herself around to peer up into his eyes. "It's the perfect date."

Smiling, she stood on tiptoe, setting a soft kiss on his lips and embracing him, feeling his body heat against her. Even in the warm summer air, the heat he was emitting was welcomed. Engulfed in his warmth, Serene lost herself to her thoughts for a moment. She, much like Ben, felt as if nothing could make this night any better.

"I'm going to miss you so much when you leave tonight," sighed Ben.

Sliding his hand down her arm, Ben laced his fingers with Serene's, leading her to the blanket he had set out. Lowering herself onto the blanket, Serene looked up to Ben who soon joined her, sitting behind her, holding her in his arms. His chest rose slowly up and down against her with each breath he took and she traced imaginary shapes and lines up and down his arms slowly. Nothing was said between them for a long time and they sat in silence with nothing but the soft chirping of the crickets to serenade them. After endless moments of stillness, Serene spoke.

"What are you thinking about?" she questioned him intently, tilting her head to look up into his eyes.

"About us. About how much I love you."

Serene froze, her mind catching up with what was just said. She didn't know how to respond and she feared the worse; she was going to cry.

Ben looked to Serene's eyes and found them glazed over as if holding back tears. For Serene, those three words caused so many mixed emotions that it took her a moment or two to gather her thoughts. Serene loved Ben. She did. There was just something missing in their relationship, something important. It was as if the foundation of their love was shaky. As if they could never be complete with one another. Of course, Ben didn't feel this, but it was a constant factor in Serene's mind.

Apparently Serene had once again fallen captive to her thoughts, because Ben spoke again.

"I love you, Serene."

Her mind raced. She wanted to pledge her love to him, but she couldn't ignore the aching feeling in the pit of her stomach. "I—I'm sorry." Tears leaked from Serene's eyes, leaving black streaks down her rosy cheeks. She simply could not bring herself to admit her love for him. Something was wrong and she feared that giving her heart to him would open her eyes to the issue, leaving her broken hearted and regretful.

Ben found himself confused and lost. Had he done something wrong? He'd been expecting Serene to return her affection for him, but instead he got apologies and tears.

"I don't understand. I—," Ben began, but was interrupted.

"I'm sorry. I can't explain. Just take me home." Training her eyes to avoid his gaze, Serene freed herself from his arms and walked back to the car, wiping her tears away quickly every few seconds.

She had gone and ruined the night, ruined her three-year anniversary, and, more then likely, ruined her relationship. Swinging the passenger seat door open, she slid in, letting out a soft sob. Peering out the window, she could see Ben gathering up the blanket and shuffling to the car. His expression would haunt her forever. Pure sadness was etched across his face.

Emotions flowed through Serene, tears sticking to her face, her hair, and her hands. The upper edge of her shirt was speckled with tear drops. As Ben opened the car door and climbed in, Serene muffled her sobs. "I'm so sorry, Ben."

"Don't be," he replied calmly, not daring to look at her in fear that his own emotions would show through, leaving him in a worse state than she was. He set the car in drive and turned it around, heading to Serene's house.

The ride seemed to last ages and the silence was eerie. Serene's heart was beating furiously, nervousness coursing through her. The once adventurous maze of streets was now taunting Serene; a never-ending map of hell. At last they pulled up outside of Serene's house. Ben sat perfectly still in his seat while Serene watched her hands.

"I—I'll call you when I get to England," said Serene with a nod before letting herself out of the car. As the door closed Ben watched her walking away.

"I love you," he whispered for only him to hear. With that, he pulled away just as Serene reached her front porch.

Pausing at the door, Serene pulled her keys and cell phone from her purse, glancing to her phone to check the time. A text message notice flashed across the screen. The message was from Hailey and it read, "How was it?"

She punched in 'horrible', hit send, and pushed the front door open.

Entering her house, she could hear someone crying. Sobbing actually. Fear shook Serene to the core. What was going on? Something was seriously wrong. Her keys clattered against the floor as she dropped her things and took off into the house, frantically searching for her mother. Was she hurt? Serene's mind ran down a check list of possibilities. Had the house been robbed? Tearing through the living room, things seemed in order. She pushed herself faster.

Sliding into the kitchen, her eyes fell on a worrisome scene.

Silvia sat hunched over at the kitchen counter, tears dripping down her face, eyeliner streaking down her cheeks. A pile of tissues sat in front of her, all of them crumpled and tear soaked. "Mom, what's wrong?" Serene walked to her mother, her fear intensifying.

"Serene," Silvia began, gathering herself as much as possible, "there's been an accident. Your father—your father is dead."

CHAPTER 3

It was as if time had stopped. Serene felt as if she had just been pushed off a very high cliff into an ocean of frigid water and jagged rocks. Her heart dropped to her stomach and a feeling of incoherence washed over her like a sheet of ice, sending waves of horror through every inch of her body. In a flash, everything she had been dreaming of, looking forward to, and waiting for was gone.

Coming to, Serene opened her mouth to speak, but nothing came out. She tried again. "What happened?" Her voice was distant, unfamiliar. Watching her mother, she waited for an answer, almost doubting that she'd get one.

"He was on his way here, to pick you up. His plane crashed. No one survived." Perhaps it was just Serene's mind playing tricks on her, but her mother's voice seemed to be stricken with a false sense of panic. Then again, her mother had just lost the only man she had ever loved. Her odd behavior was to be expected.

Taking in the new information, Serene nodded and stood in silence. What could she say or do to fix this? Nothing.

Serene stood there until she felt utterly defeated and retreated upstairs.

Entering her bedroom, Serene's blood began to boil. This was her fault. Her father had been coming to get her simply because she was constantly nagging him about never coming to see her and never keeping his promises.

"He's dead because of me," she muttered to herself, her voice low and laced with sadness, anger, and regret. She needed Ben now more than ever, but she doubted he wanted to talk to her. An aching feeling was building in her stomach. Crawling onto her bed, she curled up and began to cry. She'd never cried so much in her life.

She cried because her father was dead.

She cried because Ben's heart was broken.

She cried because her mother seemed so helpless.

But most of all, she cried because all of this, in her eyes, was her fault. Silent tears cascaded down her cheeks, dripping onto her bedspread, leaving small wet marks. She'd never be able to forgive herself for this.

How was it possible that a life, forty or so years in the making could be ended in one split moment in time? The contemplation of this sent chills of fear up and down Serene. Death had, before, only been a distant thing that she had come across in books and movies. And now it was her reality. Her life. Everything she had known to be was no longer, and this worried her. Sitting on her bed, holding her head in her hands, she felt numb. Life was not something that would be there forever. It was frail and unpredictable.

Shifting about on her bed, Serene looked to the clock on her wall. Seconds passed, and those seconds turned to minutes which, in turn, turned to hours. Still, Serene sat and watched the clock tick on, her mind whirling as the numbers crept by and, in the wee hours of the morning, she collapsed.

Curling up on her bed, sobs rang out and she muffled them with her pillow. Her father was dead. Dead. Gone forever. And there she sat, comfortable in her room, sitting her life away watching the clock.

It took her an hour of sobbing to gather herself. Sitting up, she rubbed her eyes, her mascara and eyeliner smearing even further across her face. That was it. She'd had enough.

Serene refused to sit there any longer and waste precious hours of her life. There was so much of the world to see. So many experiences to be had and she would not, unlike her friends, spend the rest of her life cramped up in her small town, living for the future. She was going to live for the day.

Standing, she stumbled over to her closet and yanked her suitcase from it. Soon, it bulged at the seams with clothing, shoes, makeup—the works. Setting it against the wall, she shuffled to her bedside table and grabbed her cell phone and purse. Setting that aside, she withdrew a small red box and set it gently on her bed. Lifting the lid, a wad of crisp green twenty dollar bills came into view. Emptying the contents of the box onto the bed, Serene plucked out all of the money she could gather and counted it carefully.

"Two-hundred eighty, three-hundred, three-hundred twenty," she counted, continuing to flick through the bills. "Three-hundred and sixty dollars." It wasn't much, but it would have to do. It was all of the birthday and Christmas money she had saved. Shoving her new found fortune into her purse, her hands retreated to the table and, reaching into the drawer once more, she pulled out a white plane ticket. It read 'Serene Valance, Flight 45 to Manchester, England. Departure: 9:00 P.M.. Seat: 15'. Reading over the ticket, she looked to the clock on the wall. Eight-fifteen, P.M.. Well, at least time was on her side for once.

Taking a few quick strides, she reached the wall and plucked up her suitcase in her right hand while clutching her purse and plane ticket in her left. As she reached the door to her room, she stole one last glance at what was formerly her home, her room, her escape. Now it was the one place she never wanted to see again. With a deep breath, she backed out of the room, gently closing the door behind her.

Tip toeing down the hall and down the stairs, she headed for the door and froze. What about her poor mother? She had just lost the only man she had ever loved and now, without so much as a warning, her only daughter was about to walk out of her life.

Serene couldn't do that to her mother.

Turning, she took a slight detour through the living room, past the pictures of she and her mother throughout the years, and into the kitchen.

Assuming she would find her mother frozen in her doubled over position, Serene opened her mouth to speak, but found an empty kitchen facing her. The mountain of tear stained tissues had since been cleared and now all that remained was a clean counter top and no evidence that a tragedy had struck this family. Taking a few more echoing steps through the kitchen, she frowned.

Had her mother gone to bed? The thought flew through Serene's mind as she spun and dashed from the kitchen. Arriving at the base of the stairs, her eyes shifted between the front door and the staircase.

Without much hesitation, she made up her mind. Grasping the chilly, silver doorknob, she yanked the door open. A gust of wind met her, blowing her hair about the frame of her face. She closed her eyes for a moment and stepped out into the night, closing the door gently behind her and giving one last saddened glance to her home.

Serene spent twenty minutes in a cab that smelled oddly with a man who spoke broken English before she reached the airport. Fifteen dollars poorer than she had been and her clothing smelling strongly of imported cigarettes, she pushed through the airport's spinning doors, catching glances from strangers as they passed through the opposite way. Holding her suitcase in one hand and desperately grasping her ticket in the other, Serene trudged to the bathroom.

The woman's room at the airport was relatively empty. There was a petite woman washing her hands at the far sink and the faint swish of a toilet flushing sounded from the third stall.

Serene paced over to one of the unoccupied sinks and set her suitcase down on the floor at her feet. She looked to the mirror and her reflection stared back at her, her big green eyes glistening with silent tears. Serene choked them back. Now was not the time to break down. She was on a journey to see the world, to find herself. How cliché. It was true, however.

Serene, who had always lived in a world where she was molded into what everyone wanted her to be, was ready to leave the person she had been forced into behind. What everyone saw wasn't Serene. The girl everyone saw was a collage of themselves. A shell that Serene was intent on riding herself of.

Breathing in and out, she looked to the clock that hung on the corner of the wall in the bathroom. Eight-forty-five. She had fifteen minutes to catch her flight. As she dashed from the bathroom, a booming voice rang out through the building.

"Flight forty-five to Manchester, England is now boarding. Flight forty-five to Manch...." Serene didn't pause to hear the rest of the announcement. Her eyes flew to the large board overhead that was flashing numbers and arrows, giving directions on which way certain flights were.

Scanning down the list, she located flight forty-five. It was in the far wing of the airport. It'd be a close call, but she'd make it if she ran. Not taking another moment to think, she turned and started off in a sprint down the airport, mumbling apologizes as her bag bumped against people in her hurry. Five minutes left. Four minutes left. Three minutes left.

With a little less than two minutes left before the flight would leave, Serene arrived at the terminal and thrust her ticket into the open hand of an overly excited flight attendant who, with a bubbly grin, spat, "Have a lovely flight!"

Serene nodded to the woman with a smile that she could only hope somewhat matched the pleasant greeting she had received.

Practically panting, Serene entered the plane and two dozen or so eyes fell on her and her seemingly panicked state. Heat rose up her neck, giving her a flushed look and she gave an embarrassed smile of sorts and directed her eyes at her feet.

Squeezing down the isle, she looked to the faces of her fellow passengers. A bald, portly little man sat aside a petite young woman. Both were laughing rather obnoxiously at whatever the plump man had just said. Three rows behind them sat a young couple holding hands. The woman clearly had a fear of flying. She was clinging to the man's hand with such strength that his fingers were slowly turning a dark shade of maroon.

Finally, glancing to the seat numbers, she came across her seat. Seat fifteen. Lifting her suitcase and standing on her toes, she reached up to the overhead compartment, trying to tuck her belongings away safely. The overhead compartment was higher up than it had appeared and Serene struggled against the weight of her suitcase, trying to cram the oversized package into the tiny compartment. Her hand slipped and with a blink of her eyes she could see her baggage making a bee line for her face. She closed her eyes and braced herself for the impact, but it never came.

"I hope you don't mind me lending a hand."

Serene opened her eyes slowly and her gaze fell on a boy, his arms reaching high above her head as he stored her luggage away with great ease. As he shut the compartment door and was sure that the bag wouldn't come tumbling down on their heads, he looked down at Serene, an enchanting smile twisting on his lips.

Serene stared in utter awe at his beauty. His skin ran flawless like porcelain; two deep, vibrant blue eyes gazed down at her. Her eyes flickered down in embarrassment as she caught herself staring and a slight hint of scarlet flushed her cheeks. Biting her lip, she gathered herself and looked back up at him. He radiated confidence matched with a hint of mystery. Smirking, he nodded at her slightly.

"Blaise Mar," he introduced himself and it took Serene a moment to respond.

"Serene Valance. Um … thanks for the help," she added with a glance to the overhead compartment that now safely concealed her luggage.

Blaise gave a small laugh and shook his head effortlessly. "Don't mention it." His eyes locked with hers and he seemed to bore into her soul with his mind numbing gaze. "You wouldn't happen to be sitting in seat fifteen, would you?" he questioned out of the blue, watching Serene intently as if her answer was the most interesting thing in the world.

Nodding, Serene glanced to her ticket simply to confirm with herself that she was, indeed, sitting in seat fifteen. Looking back up to his godly face, she nodded again.

"Yeah, seat fifteen, that's me." She glanced to her seat, a window seat—great. She already had enough issues with traveling through the air as it was. If God had wanted humans to be airborne he would have given them wings. Her gaze traveled hesitantly back to his eyes.

"Well," he began with a peek at the plane ticket grasped in his hand, "it seems we are flying partners." His grin held strong, showing of his perfect teeth.

Serene felt a pang of excitement flood her body. She tried to stifle it. Despite her sudden plan to run away, she didn't want to forget all about Ben. She wondered if he cared enough to worry about her when she was found missing by her mother in the morning. Shoving the thought aside, she focused on Blaise who glanced to his seat and back to Serene.

"If everyone could please take their seats before takeoff, we will be departing momentarily," the flight attendant's perky voice sang out over the intercom, causing many wandering passengers to scuttle to their seats in a frenzy. Serene slid into her row, past Blaise's seat and into her own, pulling down the window curtain quickly. Blaise must have noticed because he gave a low chuckle.

"Not a frequent flyer I take it?" he questioned, smiling warmly at her as he slid into his seat beside her, buckling up in a flash.

Shaking her head, Serene smiled shyly. "Not exactly."

In fact, this was Serene's first time flying. She somehow felt much more at ease about the entire situation with Blaise there. Perhaps it would be nice having him as a friend to chat with on the way to England. Of course, that was assuming that she found the nerve to string together an entire sentence without fumbling over words.

"It's not all that bad," he assured her with a glance to the front of the plane. It was then that Serene noted he had an accent—British. She assumed he was going home then. It was beyond her why anyone would travel to Covington. There wasn't that much to grovel over, not in comparison to England anyway.

"Did you come here on vacation?" she questioned, hoping it would make for an easy conversation starter.

"I suppose you could say that," he replied with a smile, steeling a glance toward the cockpit as if anxious to take off.

Serene was anything but anxious to be hurdling through the sky in a large heap of metal, but she had her mind set on escaping the town, the state, even the country. Waiting for him to elaborate his answer, she took a few deep breaths, trying to calm her nerves. She looked to Blaise who appeared to be preparing to continue his answer, but he was cut off by the sudden rumble shaking through the plane.

Serene immediately locked her eyes on the back of the seat in front of her, trying with all her might not to lose it. As the aircraft picked up speed, the vibration of the plane intensified. The plane began to lift off the runway and head to the sky.

Serene released a small whimper and latched her hand down on the arm rest, quickly snatching it back as she realized Blaise's hand already occupied it. An awkward moment passed after Serene grasped onto Blaise's hand before he broke the silence with a low laugh and smile.

Serene, who was too busy breathing, ignored him for the time being and focused her thoughts on surviving takeoff. Breathing in and out, she glanced over to Blaise and mustered a weak smile.

"I'm not usually this much of a wimp," she admitted through gritted teeth. This was true. Serene was not known for being stricken with fear all that often. She liked to think of herself as a strong-willed individual.

Shaking his head, he gave a comforting grin.

"Don't worry about," his smooth voice chimed. It was music to Serene's ears. Putting things in perspective, her mind raced furiously. She was on the way out of the hell hole that was formerly her home, she was in a plane on her way to England—a place she had never been before—and her flight partner was God's perfection of the male species. Compared to what she had just suffered through, this was like heaven.

"Flying to England with your family?" Blaise's voice broke her thoughts and she looked over to him as if it was an odd question. It donned on her that he was unaware that she was flying solo and of the fact that there was no plural 'parents'. Her father was dead.

"Oh, no. I'm flying alone," she stated, her voice nearly cracking as she recovered from her pre-flight jitters.

As the plane leveled in the sky and set on its path to England, the flight attendants began their rounds. "Would you care for a drink?" asked a young brunette woman clad in her stylish flight attendant outfit.

Serene was feeling a bit parched, probably from her excessive intake of deep breaths. She nodded warily. "Water," she blurted out, "please," she rushed, tacking on the end bit for politeness. The woman turned her gaze on Blaise. He simply shook his head graciously and traced figures absentmindedly on his jeans. It was then, as the flight attendant sauntered off to retrieve Serene's water, that she was able to take in Blaise's figure.

He was strong, muscular, yet had a lanky build that would surely allow him to tower over her. Muscles ripped down his arms which were cleverly revealed by his tight, fitted t-shirt. A pair of faded blue jeans adorned his lower body. Clothing looked nice on him. It probably looked even nicer off of him.

A wave of fatigue came over Serene. She blamed this on the horrific day she had just suffered through. Dimming her overhead light, she glanced to Blaise. She wanted so badly to talk to him. Shifting to a more comfortable position, she watched him for a moment and he looked to her.

"What's England like?" she questioned in hopes of sparking further conversation with him. "Cold and wet," he answered with the smallest of smiles. How anyone could smile at that was beyond Serene. England was beginning to seem less appealing.

A few more questions were exchanged and she learned that he was born in Manchester, England and had lived there his entire life, but was frequently traveling. He lived with a few friends in a small house they chipped in to pay for and he was currently single. Butterflies flittered in Serene's stomach. She also learned that he was a year older than she and would be attending a small college on the outskirts of Manchester.

He questioned her as well, learning of her father's recent death at which he lent sympathy and condolence, eyeing her warily as if she might go postal at any moment. However, Serene seemed to have her wits about her—more than a person who just lost their father should. Shock, perhaps?

An hour or so wore by and Serene's fatigue never lessened. She recalled at one point shifting a pillow beneath her head and listening to Blaise's melodic voice which seemingly lulled her to sleep.

"You look exhausted," were the last words Serene grasped before slipping into slumber.

CHAPTER 4

A loud boom of laughter shook Serene from her sleep and, shifting, she rubbed at her eyes, gazing around before daring to peek out the window.

It seemed to be daytime, but she wasn't sure what time it was. Should she be using American time or England's time? Either way, she'd gotten a good amount of sleep. The laugh that had awoken her came from none other than the portly little man she had eyed at the beginning of her voyage.

Looking over, Blaise wasn't there. That was peculiar, but it didn't faze her. How far could someone get on an airplane? The question was immediately answered as Blaise swiftly plopped down into his seat, smiling at her. "Sleep well?" he asked, his stunningly charming British accent positively melting from his words.

"Surprisingly, yes," she responded, shocked that she had slept so well—considering that she was thousands of feet above the ground, her life hanging in the hands of the plane and its pilot.

It hadn't struck Serene until now that perhaps her sudden fear of flying was induced by her father's death just hours ago—in a plane crash. For reasons beyond her imagination, she was yet to truly mourn her father's death, save for her small moment of weakness in her bedroom just after hearing the news. It wasn't that she didn't love Luther. She loved him, of course, but he'd rarely been there for her. There was—or had been—an icy distance between them. A never fading wall of glares and regret had, over the years, built up between Serene and her father. And, despite her numerous attempts, nothing ever worked out the way she planned it. This didn't merely relate to Luther either. Nothing worked out for her, period. Her friends were marginal at best and she had, hours ago, shattered the heart of the only person that ever seemed to portray a glimpse of undying loyalty toward her.

"Told ya that it wouldn't be that bad." Blaise's features twisted into a grin. He was right though, it wasn't that bad. Not as bad as Serene had made it out to be. Although, she had her reasons.

He shifted in his seat, adjusting so he had a better view of her. His eyes took her in. Her long, flowing brown hair that was slightly curled at the ends, her sultry green eyes that could light up a room, her small, almost shy smile that curved gently in the corners of her lips, and her skin—smooth and flawless with a small touch of red on her cheeks where her blood coursed rapidly with every small embarrassment. Blaise twitched uncomfortably in his seat and his eyes stole a quick glance down her body. She was petite, but had all the features of a young adult.

Catching his gaze, Serene felt her face flush with anger—no—nervousness. Blaise noted her blush filled cheeks and laughed to himself. She hurriedly rushed on, searching for a topic of discussion that would keep his eyes locked with hers. If only so she could stare at him for just a second longer.

"Who did you say you lived with again?" she questioned, although she recalled perfectly well that he lived with several friends.

"Well," he began, his accent running heavily with his words, "there's Damian Carali—he and I have been friends forever. Then there's Hayden Mave who's like a brother to me, and Alaria Zoraida, Hayden's girlfriend. Of course, we are all pretty much a family." He nodded, watching Serene closely. She nodded and smiled in return. It sounded like so much fun to live with a small group of close-knit friends.

"What about you?" he asked. "Where are you traveling to? And why alone?"

Taking a deep sigh, Serene tried to find the words to explain her situation.

"I … ran away." Yes, that suited the situation nicely.

"From?" Blaise asked with a furrowed eyebrow as if she was making some ghastly mistake and that she'd be doomed to hell later for it.

"Life. My old life. I need a new life."

Life seemed to have a lot to do with everything these days. It just wasn't fair that some got to live such easy, simple lives, while the rest of the world trudged through every ghastly day, barely believing it when they awoke the next morning to find that there wasn't any fire and brimstone rocketing from beneath the earth outside their houses.

Serene mustered the best smile she could. "It's okay though, really. I'll be fine. I'm just going to explore the world." She stated this like it was some mediocre task, as if it were quite normal for teenage girls to be running off to foreign countries without any fear in the world.

"What about your friends? Your mom? Your boyfriend?"

Friends. Mom. Boyfriend. Serene ran these words through her head and froze for a moment before looking to him with a shrug.

"My friends will manage without me. My mom will—I don't know. And—I don't have a boyfriend." Her last words were forced out with such agony that she was sure it showed.

Blaise seemed perplexed by this. It was as if he had been expecting a different answer.

Well, that was that. Serene had unofficially ended things with Ben. A small portion of her felt a deep sigh of agony, while the rest of her seemed oddly delighted, as if this had been a decision she had been persuading her inner self to make for some time now.

She couldn't place it, but something inside Serene was changing. She didn't know if it was a repercussion of finding new places and new people or the death of her father, but she was changing. Not only her life, but herself as well. A new found confidence was kindled within her, the flames licking up higher and higher as time passed.

"Well, I hope that all works out for you. Your new life and everything."

"Thanks," she muttered graciously and looked to the small analog clock built into the screen at the front of the plane. Eleven A.M.—in Manchester. If Serene was doing that math right, adding in the time difference, it had been about six hours since takeoff.

"Only two more hours," she breathed, more to herself than to Blaise.

"Anxious to land?" His question didn't need an answer. Smirking, he leaned toward Serene slightly, his arm just brushing hers.

"You know, with all that worrying you do, it's no wonder you blush so much." He grinned and locked eyes with her for a moment before leaning back in his respected seat, leaving Serene with the feeling that she had missed something. Whatever it was, she didn't care. Being so close to Blaise was exhilarating, and the fact that he noticed how often she blushed simply caused her to redden even more, her cheeks turning florid.

Landing was quite a different experience from the smooth sailing she had just endured. The plane shook violently as they went into a downward nose dive, the ground quickly rising to meet them. Serene was sure, for a moment, that this was the end. In a moment she'd be an insignificant splatter on the landing strip. Her knuckles turned white as she clenched the arm rests on either side of her with great force. Not even the Jaws of Life could pry her from the flimsy plastic arm rests that could, potentially, keep her from flying face first into the seat in front of her. She could hear the faint chuckling of Blaise beside her. She took a breath and stole a glance at him. He was watching her with a sparkling gaze and a smirk.

"What's so funny?" she hissed through clenched teeth.

"Look at yourself. You'd think that we were falling to our imminent doom or something rather than simply landing a plane," he teased. In a flash, he reached out with one perfectly sculpted hand and set it softly atop hers, fixing his eyes on her.

His hand was smooth against her skin and Serene immediately eased her tension on the arm rest. Her palm turned up slightly to meet his and her eyes fell down to her hand overlapped by his.

His hand was much larger in comparison to hers and his skin was a tad bit paler, but still perfect. His hand felt slightly chilled against hers, but she was so overheated that it hardly fazed her.

The plane shook violently once again as they grew nearer to the black tar stretching out endlessly ahead of them. Serene's muscles tensed up and, catching her sudden apprehension, Blaise laced his fingers with hers, his gaze never leaving her eyes, as if to say that everything would be fine. Serene believed him. His eyes held a truth that didn't compare to anything she had ever witnessed before and she couldn't help but find herself lost in his icy stare. Their bodies both began to lean toward one another, their faces slowly inching closer and closer. Without Serene's awareness, she suddenly found her lips a mere inch from Blaise's. Heat quickly crept up her neck, overwhelming her, her blood rushing anxiously through her body.

Blaise's eyes shot to her neck and back to her eyes so quickly that Serene barely noticed. With great hesitation, he leaned back and smirked at her. The sudden temptation of a kiss just out of reach lingered on her lips, her heart pulsing away in her chest. Nothing had happened, but part of her wished it had. She evaded her gaze to the window. In her moment of desire, she hadn't realized that the plane had landed. Her hand was still firmly laced with Blaise's, but her other hand no longer grasped the arm rest. It sat gently on her lap, feeling left out.

"That landing wasn't so bad, eh?" He smirked, his eyes glinting with a spark that made Serene wondered if that had all been a charade to keep her mind off of the difficult landing and focused on his heavenly features instead. Whatever it was—it worked.

"Enjoyable, actually," she replied with a devious smile. Turning her eyes reluctantly to the window, she lifted the window shade up and peered out. It was gray, cloudy, and steadily misting on the inhabitants of Manchester, England. Serene had read once that it rained quite often in most areas of England. This hadn't bothered her before her arrival, but she wasn't sure her sunny weathered clothing would fare well in such a wet environment.

"Everyone may now safely depart from the aircraft. I hope you enjoyed your flight," rang the warm voice of the flight attendant. Everyone slowly rose from their seats, stretching out in ever direction and grasping at the air for the overhead compartments. Before Serene could do much of anything, Blaise reached up and popped open the compartment, gracefully pulling Serene's suitcase out and turning, walking down the aisle and off the plane.

Serene was never so grateful to feel cold, solid concrete unmoving beneath her feet. Smiling down graciously at the gray slates, she silently thanked them for existing.

Blaise had escorted Serene off the plane, through the terminal and out of the overly crowded airport. He led her to the front parking lot, carrying her luggage the entire way despite her protest. The pair now stood just outside the airport, Serene gazing lovingly at the ground while Blaise tried to scope out a taxi.

Serene emerged from her stupor. Feeling like an unwanted burden, she pried her luggage from Blaise's grasp. The sky was still misting, spitting warm droplets of water on Serene, causing her hair to gradually curl up. She hurriedly tried to tame her hair, running her hands through it repeatedly while feeling overwhelmingly self conscious. She narrowed her gaze against the drizzle and peered around the lot.

It donned on Serene that she had missed a major flaw in her runaway plan—shelter, of which she had none. She would have stayed with her father, but that plan was shot to hell. Now what was she to do?

She only had a few hundred dollars left. Not enough to rent an apartment or even a hotel room for that matter. Going back wasn't an option either; she didn't have enough money for a return ticket. Great. Her mind worked overtime to remedy the situation, but she wasn't having any luck.

"Want to share a cab?"

Blaise's voice surprised her and she quickly looked up. Share a cab? Well, she didn't see anything wrong with the suggestion, except for the fact that she didn't know where she was going. Not knowing what to tell him, she simply nodded and glanced around.

Blaise waved his hand in the air, giving a sharp whistle and within seconds a yellow car came to an abrupt halt, inches from Serene's toes. She gave a nervous gasp and smiled weakly over at Blaise. He set his hand on her shoulder, opening the cab's door for her and helping her in. He slid in after her, closing the door and glancing to the front seat. His eyes shifted cautiously to Serene for a moment before he turned to the driver, muttering his desired destination, his words inaudible to her ears. Shrugging it off, she stared blankly out the window as the cab pulled away from the airport. Well, the hard part of her trip was over. She had made it to England in one piece. That was saying something.

The drive from the airport to Blaise's house was short, too short. She mentally slapped herself for keeping so silent. For all she knew, this could be the last time she would ever talk to him and she hadn't even gotten his number yet.

As the cab pulled up to his house, he sifted through his pocket and handed a small gathering of coins to the driver, muttering 'thank you' before turning his beautiful blue eyes on Serene.

"Where should I tell him to take you?" he questioned, a clever smile replacing his usual smirk.

"Well, actually—I don't have anywhere to stay," she muttered, trying to shrug it off as if it were nothing. Blaise cocked an eyebrow at her.

"Running away from home, no place to stay, and I'm guessing you didn't bring a fortune with you." He laughed lightly, despite the situation Serene was facing. It didn't seem to faze him a bit. Serene took this slightly offensively.

"Well, I'm sure I can manage just fine, thanks," she scoffed, rolling her eyes.

"Perhaps."

He pushed open the car door and half of his body emerged onto to the cloudy street. His motions held a strong sense of hesitation that made Serene watch him intensely.

"Hey …" he hesitated, looking over his shoulder at her and then to the front door of the house. With a sigh of defeat that Serene couldn't understand, he looked back to her once more. "You can stay with me. If you want too, that is."

Something in his voice made Serene think that there was some underlying reason that he wanted her to turn down the offer, but his eyes told a different story. He seemed to genuinely want her to stay with him, but something was bothering him.

"Oh, no, that's okay. I don't want to be—"

"You're not a burden. You don't have anywhere to stay and I'm sure I'm the only Brit you know, so why not?" His striking eyes locked with hers, intensifying his words.

That was all the persuasion Serene needed. Quickly grabbing her suitcase, she clambered out of the car, shut the door, and walked to the sidewalk where Blaise stood, waiting. Her eyes turned to the cab as it pulled away. Well, having no way of leaving now, she was forced to accept the offer.

Her mind suddenly snapped to a thought.

Blaise lived with his friends. That meant that she too would be residing with his friends, without their prior knowledge or approval. Her heart dropped to her stomach, her insides twisting in anxious knots. Maybe this wasn't such a great idea.

"Blaise, I really don't want to bother your friends," she began, but he cut her off, shaking his head and smiling.

"Don't be silly. I'm sure they'd love to meet you," he coaxed. "Don't worry about it."

Serene gave an uncommitted smile and curved her eyes to the front door.

The wooden tiles seemed to form a disdainful grin, glowering at her as if many secrets were withheld behind its timber frame. Looking up, the house towered three stories above her. It was an old, Victorian styled manor, red bricks accented with deep wooden windows, shades pulled tightly over them. The house looked thriving, yet somehow vacant. Perhaps it was due to the weather. Rain and clouds could make even the happiest of places appear dreary.

Rocking on the souls of her feet, she took a tentative step back as Blaise grasped the brass doorknob, turning it with ease. Giving the door an agile push, the hinges whined in complaint, as if the door was seldom used.

Blaise motioned to the doorway, signaling for Serene to enter first.

After a moment of hesitation that seemed to drag on forever, she swallowed her nerves and stepped over the threshold. Entering the house, the door shut behind her, a sickening darkness covering the room, leaving Serene blinded. Instantly her muscles clenched, her teeth gnashed, and the fine hairs on the back of her neck stood on end. Straining her ears, she could hear Blaise behind her, his breathing shaky, uneven.

Footsteps echoed softly from the corner of the room, falling harder against the floor as the person neared. Serene balled her hands into fists, paranoia getting the best of her. Blaise shuffled quickly behind her and the room unexpectedly flooded with light. An aching pain immediately throbbed behind Serene's eyes as she adjusted to the abrupt luminosity. Her gaze fell on three figures. A boy and a girl sitting gracefully in chairs against the far wall set their piercing eyes on her, and another boy, the eldest by the looks of him, was striding toward her, a disgruntled look twisting on his features.

His eyes shot above her head, locking with Blaise's no doubt, before snapping back to Serene. The two in the chairs looked on eagerly. The eldest boy came to a halt five feet from Serene and, as his displeased look melted into a grin, Serene gasped.

Two, sharp fangs gleamed at her from beneath the boy's crimson lips.

CHAPTER 5

A devilish spark gleamed in his eyes, his piercing stare never flinching from Serene's face. He was magnificent in appearance. Copper locks of hair were strewn in perfect chaos atop his head, hanging delicately in front of two, brown eyes that seemed to be circled in blood red. He towered over Serene by a good foot or so, his head tilted down to her.

His eyes scrutinized the length of her body, checking for any damage done to his goods. Serene cringed back in terror, a sudden realization coursing through her. Blaise's awareness of her blushing as blood reddened her skin; the dark, damp state of the house; the two, glistening fangs, smirking at her mockingly. These people were not people at all.

They were vampires.

In a frantic, sickening moment of panic, she took a rapid step back, preparing to make a run for it, but as she spun around her body slammed into something hard; something stone solid. Her gaze lifted up into the face of Blaise, standing defensively in front of her, blocking her path and hindering her escape. Hastily, she backed away from him, her eyes brimming with tears. This could not be happening. She had trusted Blaise. Even worse, she had begun to like him, and he had betrayed her.

This was insane. Vampires weren't real. They were fictional monsters; creatures of the night that sucked the blood of their victims who were generally naive females, lured unknowingly into their trap.

Now that she thought about it, if Blaise and his friends really were vampires, she had just nominated herself as the naive female. But how was this possible? There wasn't a single logical idea that could prove that vampires existed and captured victims. It was ridiculous, idiotic, and outlandish.

And it had just happened to Serene.

"I—Blaise—..." Serene stammered, trying to find something to say, something that didn't sound completely bizarre or frightened, in case all of this was some big joke.

Blaise peered down, towering over her. His eyes held a peculiar mixture of pain, pleasure, and remorse. He parted his lips, preparing to speak, but nothing happened. Finding himself speechless, he lowered his stare in shame.

She hadn't seen any fangs on Blaise. Maybe he wasn't a vampire. Maybe he just worked for them, as a slave of sorts, trading victims in return for his own life.

"What's your name?"

A velvet, crystalline voice sung out from behind Serene. Fear was numbing ever inch of her body, threatening to leave her frozen there, in the watchful gaze of at least once vampire. She couldn't be too sure about the others. She'd have to see their fangs. It was the only conformation required for her eyes.

Turning cautiously toward the voice, she practically held her breath, in fear that they all might hear her shaky breathing and assess her as an easy, frightened meal. Goose bumps dotted her arms and legs as the boy took a step toward her, seemingly gliding rather than walking. His motions were so smooth and precise that it was hard to catch him in the act. After a moment of dead silence, the boy spoke again.

"What is your name, girl?" he inquired again, a hint of irritation obvious in his voice.

"Serene," she retorted, trying her hardest to portray nothing but bravery.

"Serene," he repeated. "A lovely name. However, it doesn't suit you. You see Serene, 'serene' means tranquil, calm—of which you are neither. Not currently at any rate. I suggest you calm down. The faster your heart beats, the more alluring the smell of your blood is, so warm and thick, coursing just beneath a few layers of delicate mortal flesh."

A queasy sensation churned in Serene's stomach, her vision going foggy for a moment as she struggled against her senses to prevent herself from passing out. The last thing she wanted was to crash at the feet of a blood craving vampire.

"I'm Hayden. And these two are-" he motioned to the boy and the girl perched effortlessly in their chairs.

"Damian and Alaria," Serene ended his sentence with a pleased grin of her own.

"I see that Blaise has filled you in nicely." Hayden's eyes snapped to Blaise, an icy glare sending unheard threats.

A motion from the corner of the room caught Serene's attention. Alaria had risen from her seat and was now sauntering to Hayden's side, a defiant stare transfixed on her visage. She too radiated a godly perfection, but her appearance was darker than the others. Lengthy black hair cascaded down her back, framing her face nicely. Striking silver eyes seemed to catch every ray of light that hit them, giving her gaze an icy glow.

Arriving at Hayden's side, she linked her arm with his, turning her eyes on Serene, taking in the small token that Blaise had lured to them. Her pale pink lips parted delicately, revealing her own pair of jagged teeth, as she spoke in whispers to Hayden. After a long moment, she turned to Blaise.

"What is the meaning of this, Blaise?" Alaria questioned, her voice sharper than Hayden's, distinct fury evident in her tone.

"She didn't have anywhere to stay."

"So you assumed you'd bring her back here and that would be alright? She is mortal, Blaise. Nothing more than dinner for us." Alaria's glare sharpened considerably.

"We can't kill her. This is my fault. Let's just let her go," Blaise pleaded, his eyes softening with his voice.

Serene stood frozen in irrefutable fear, listening intently to the conversation taking place before her. Something about the conversation seemed unreal. The entire situation was leaving Serene with no sense of reality.

Hours ago she had been enjoying her meager conversation with Blaise and now she stood, listening as two vampires argued over her impending death.

"Let her go? Let her go? You've lost your mind, Blaise. We all could be put in unimaginable danger because of your foolish antics."

"Enough!" Hayden broke in, instantaneously impeding the conflict between the two. "Damian," he hissed, his glare snapping to the third male who had remained mute since Serene's arrival, "take Serene to the office. Restrain her there until we figure out what to do with our delicate guest."

Damian rose from his chair, revealing him to be the tallest in the immediate vicinity. It was apparent that he was the youngest of the group, looking to be about a year older than Serene. Clad in a black, form fitted tee, his muscles ripped down his arms and torso. Hair black as night hung in a shaggy, tousled mess, veiling his eyes.

With a few swift strides, he was at Serene's side, locking his grasp on her shoulder and forcefully pulling her away from Blaise and past Hayden and Alaria, his eyes never leaving the ground.

When the others were long down the hall and out of ear shot, Damian loosened his death grip on Serene's shoulder and she shrugged slightly, relieved as blood returned to the previously clenched skin. The forced pushes stopped and he gently guided her down the darkened hallway, his features barely visible in the bleak conditions.

Coming to an abrupt halt, he turned, quickly pushing the door to his right open and dragging Serene in before shutting the door. Sliding his hand down her arm and taking a firm grip on her wrist, he drug her further into the room.

Serene, shaking with fear, took a panicked look around.

The room was dark, much like the rest of the house, and the walls were lined with shelves, piled to the ceiling with books, many so old that they appeared to be from other centuries. Dust coated many surfaces in the room, making it evident that it was hardly, if ever, used. A small desk sat in the center of the room, a window above it with drapes pulled shut. Being here made Serene cringe and the prospect of what might happen to her here made her cringe even more.

Grabbing the rickety, wooden chair from behind the desk, Damian shook off the dust and slammed it down on its four wooden peg legs in the center of the room, vehemently shoving Serene down on it with a commanding grasp.

Squinting, Serene could see Damian moving quickly to the desk. With a soft click, a yellow glow flooded the room, giving Serene a better look at him. He was even more glorious in the golden halo of light. As Serene watched him, he sifted through the top drawer of the desk. She got the feeling that, through his curtain of black locks, he was watching her. Running was not an option, unless she wanted to face a painful and untimely death.

It didn't matter. Before she could so much as think of running, Damian was in front of her, his hands moving quickly, bounding her with rope that he must have fetched from the desk. The line cut into her skin, irritating it and leaving red marks. She squirmed, willing him to stop, but he continued, pulling tighter at the cords. Finishing it off with an impossibly complex knot, he sighed, glaring at the floor. Serene let out the smallest of whimpers and Damian's head shot up, his eyes locking with hers.

Awe struck, Serene's mind slipped from the pain in her bound body and focused on Damian's eyes. They were a dark shade of violet and, catching off the light on the desk, they seemed to sparkle, leaving Serene in an amazed stupor.

"Sorry." His voice was filled with a shame that Serene couldn't understand. It made her think that he didn't want this to happen, that he was different from the others.

Before she could respond, he stood and turned, moving swiftly from the room without a second glance back.

Serene found herself alone now, her previous shock and astonishment subsiding, being replaced with a chilling terror.

"Wake up, Serene. Wake up." Convinced that she had fallen asleep on the plane and was dreaming, she tried to awaken herself, to release herself from the fear that was slowly drowning her. Nothing happened and the realization that this was reality and not a dream was slowly sinking in, filling her with dread. Hot tears began to puddle up in her eyes, fogging her vision before they spilled over, trailing down her face.

The ropes were bound so tightly that she had less than a quarter of an inch of movement. Choking back sobs, Serene began to twist her wrists painfully against the rugged cords. The more she struggled, the deeper they pressed into her skin, threatening to cut her. She knew that, even if she screamed, no one would come. No one would hear her. Straining her ears, she could hear the muffled voices of the gathering just down the hall. Time was crucial and Serene was quickly running out of the precious commodity.

Quick thinking was necessary. Raised voices were echoing down the hall now, but she couldn't make out what was being said. Wriggling against the strain of the ropes, she clenched her teeth, trying to fight off the searing pain caused by her constricting binds. Maybe, if she moved just a bit more, she could undo her hands and release herself. Twisting her hands upwards from behind her back, she scratched at the ropes, desperately trying to untie the knots. Working her finger in between two sections of rope, she tugged repeatedly, feeling the knot beginning to loosen gradually as she worked at it.

Moments passed, flying by at a rapid pace. Serene wasn't sure exactly how much time she had spent working at the knots, but she was almost certain that she had little time left before someone came to fetch her. Her fingers worked rapidly, scratching and yanking at the hemp ropes that were just about loose enough to free herself. She was mere inches of rope away from freedom. One more sharp tug and the ropes would fall gracefully to the floor. Her only problem then would be to escape the morbid house unseen and unheard, a task that might be more difficult than escaping her cord prison.

The thumping sound of boots against the floor came thudding down the hall toward Serene. Heart racing and tremors of fear rattling her body, she hesitantly looked up. A dead silence encased the room; Serene's heart pounded vigorously in her ears.

With a steady, deliberate motion, the doorknob began to turn.

CHAPTER 6

The door creaked open slowly, flooding the hall with the faint glimmer of light coming from the desk lamp. Blaise's tall figure was outlined in the doorway, his movements quick, sharp, and filled with frustration—a residue from the argument. His gaze fell gently on Serene, pity vibrating from him. Narrowing her eyes to a glare, Serene turned her face stubbornly to the right, concentrating on the wall.

Heaving a bothered sigh, Blaise paced toward her, his feet padding against the wooden floorboards. Serene refused to meet his unflinching stare. She would not beg for mercy nor go down without a fight. Her mind was already working hastily, plotting away some means of escape. The wall was blank, giving Serene little to hold her gaze on. Suddenly, an icy finger trailed down her cheek, coming to a rest on her chin. The pressure of the finger against her chin forced her head forward, her eyes locking on Blaise, who was now kneeling in front of her, his eyes at her level. Clenching her teeth, she glowered defiantly at him.

"I'm sorry, Serene. I didn't mean for this to happen." His voice was tender, soothing, like a lullaby to her ears. "We voted on what to do with you. Alaria wants you dead, but

Damian and I voted against her. Hayden doesn't know, or doesn't care. Whichever the case, you're alive—for now," he muttered, trying desperately to make his words inaudible to her ears, trying not to upset her.

Alive for now. That was hardly comforting, but she supposed it was better than getting her blood sucked dry right this very moment. Balling her hands into fists behind her back, she gnashed her teeth and nodded.

"Fine, now let me go," she seethed, venomous anger lacing her words. "Please," she added, trying to give herself more of a damsel in distress attitude, for her own sake.

"I'll untie you, but you must promise me you won't run. Trust me, I'd love to let you go, but Alaria will have you dead in seconds if she thinks you're going to run."

His eyes kept focus on hers, being sure to make his words perfectly clear. Any mishaps and Serene would be his dinner, with or without her consent. Serene nodded, showing that she comprehended what he was saying and promising to follow his rules, even if she didn't mean it. Betrayal must have radiated from her eyes.

"I mean it Serene. It's your funeral. I've already had mine." A smirk twisted on his lips and he shifted the chair, giving him better access to the last knots keeping her bound to the wooden rods. "I see you've been working at these. Impressive. They aren't easy knots to undo and, by the looks of it, you were almost there. Though, one of us would have caught your scent before you even made it down the hall."

Great. Not only was she being watched with extreme caution, but even if she did attempt to escape, they could simply sniff her out, like wolves hunting their prey. The cord that had been cutting her skin loosened further still and finally dropped to the floor, landing with a hushed smack.

Standing quickly, her knees quivered as her body weight was suddenly forced on them after sitting for so long. The ground quickly began to rise up as Serene toppled toward the floor. Before she knew what had happened, her feet were planted firmly on the floor, a steady hand keeping her held upright. Blaise stood at her side, grinning as he assisted her in remaining balanced.

"Come on, I'll take you out to the others."

She hesitated and reluctantly followed him out of the office and back down the darkened hall. "It's too dark in here."

"You get use to it after a while."

Serene didn't know much about vampires, but judging from what she had gathered from movies, a while to a vampire could mean hundreds, if not thousands, of years. Part of her secretly prayed that Blaise wasn't hundreds of years old. Despite the fact that he had kidnaped her, he was still godly and made Serene's heart skip a beat. Crushing on a one-hundred year old vampire hadn't been on her summer's to-do list. However, Serene had much larger problems to deal with. Confined in a dark manor occupied by a gathering of vampires was currently the most pressing matter.

Serene was sure that her mother would be worried sick by now, no doubt sending out a search team to recover her lost daughter. Ben would have heard of her father's death and be wondering where she was as well, likely enlisting Melissa and Hailey to help search the town and neighboring areas. Serene wondered how long it would take her mom to find her suitcase and plane ticket missing and deduce that she had run off to England on her own free will.

Would it be too late by then? Would they find Serene dead in a dark alley somewhere in Manchester, drained of all of her blood, pale as a ghost? The thought unnerved Serene, causing her to dive bomb back into reality and look around with caution.

The living room glowed with a soft, yellow light, radiating from two lamps positioned strategically in two corners of the room. Hayden and Alaria sat on a smooth black couch at the far end of the room, conversing in hushed mutters. Alaria glanced up quickly as Blaise and Serene entered. Instinctively, Serene took a significant step back, intent on keeping as much space as possible between she and her female adversary.

Slowly, Alaria leaned into Hayden, their lips touching briefly before she rose, casting a cruel glare at Serene. With swift strides, she departed from the room, passing quickly by Serene, a look of utter distaste clouding her features.

"You'll have to forgive her. She's taking this harder than I anticipated."

Serene looked to Hayden, who was now rising to greet her properly. It was peculiar, watching him behave this way. His appearance masked him as a young adult, perhaps twenty years old at most, but his dialect was mature, perhaps that of a middle-aged man. It was a formality that could only have been acquired in years of experience and knowledge of previous time eras.

"Please, sit. There's much to discuss," directed Hayden.

With gentle nudges from Blaise, Serene padded across the room to the couch where Hayden reseated himself, waiting. Motioning to the couch cushion beside him, Hayden smiled, his warm grin corrupted by his two lethal fangs. Serene tentatively perched next to him, sitting on the edge of her seat, ready to make a dash for the door if need be. Blaise lounged comfortably in a chair just opposite the couch.

"I'm sure you have many questions. Don't be afraid to ask."

Serene swallowed and nodded. Questions bounced around madly in her head, causing complete chaos in her thoughts and giving her a throbbing headache. Gathering herself, she started with her most imperative question.

"Why aren't you guys attacking me right now? How are you so controlled?"

A low grumble of laughter shook through Hayden and Blaise at once, sending chills up Serene's spine.

"Common misconception. We aren't savages, searching frantically, day and night, for someone to attack. We drink when we need too," Blaise answered casually, leaning back in his chair.

"So, you don't drink human blood?"

"Yes, we do, just not as often as you'd think. An average vampire only needs to feed every four days or so. We generally drink a bit and save the rest of the blood for later use—to keep the killing to a minimum." Hayden's eyes watched Serene with intent interest. Either that, or he was keeping a close eye on her, incase she tried to run.

"You just kill innocent people?" Her eyes widened in horror at the prospect of innocent people being sucked to death.

"It's our only means of survival Serene. We only kill those we deem worthy of being killed; criminals, predators. We don't kill the good, just the bad."

She bit her lip. Well, at least it wasn't as bad as she had thought originally. They didn't kill for pleasure, but rather for survival, and they were resourceful, saving blood from previous victims for later consumption. It was apparent that their way of living had been carefully thought out, making sure not to leave any trail of their existence.

"Have any of you ever, you know, lost it?"

"And killed somebody for pleasure? It's known to happen, Serene, which is partially why we are so hesitant to allow you to stay here. Your own safety is at risk. Alaria, however, is more concerned about the well-being of our covenant, rather than your protection. I assume you are aware that if we feel threatened by you or believe you will betray our secret to the world we will have little choice but to be rid of you. That is how it must be handled. Do you understand?"

Nodding furiously, Serene bit the inside of her lip. Her life had suddenly gone from slightly unpredictable to a complete black hole of unknown fate. One wrong move and she'd find her neck in the mouth of a blood lusting vampire. The thought made her shudder.

"How did all of this start? How did you all become vampires?"

"I sired Alaria four centuries ago. She, in turn, sired Blaise who, sixty-eight years ago, sired Damian. He is the youngest of us." Hayden's gaze shifted to Blaise before returning to Serene.

"So, who changed you?" she inquired, her eyes glued to Hayden.

"A woman I met when I was twenty. I haven't seen her since the night she bit me," Hayden responded, leaving an air of mystery lingering in the room.

Soft thuds echoed from down the hall, infiltrating the living room and steadily growing louder. Damian's built shadow appeared at the mouth of the living room. Light crept slowly up his body as he paced into the room until the soft glow showered his entire figure. His head hung slightly, just as it had before, his brilliant violet eyes shrouded by his black veil of hair. His muscular shape was even more prominent in the light as he moved toward them.

"Hayden, Blaise," he muttered, nodding to each of them respectively and disregarding Serene. Shifting uncomfortably next to Hayden, her eyes seemed transfixed on Damian, wondering what his intense issue was with her. She knew that Alaria wanted her dead, but Damian had voted to keep her alive, so why was his attitude toward her so disgruntled?

"Hi Damian." Serene's voice quivered with uncertainty, her gaze instantly falling to her lap as her words came out uncertain.

A simple head nod was all she received from the profound boy, his gaze still secreted.

"Alaria's gone," breathed Damian, his deep voice never faltering.

"Gone? Where did she go?" Hayden questioned, rising swiftly from his seat, advancing on Damian with agile movements.

"She said she's going to Russia until *she*," he motioned to Serene, "leaves." His voice was sharp like a razor. It pained Serene to hear Damian speak of her with such disdain in his tone.

"Russia? Fine. If you hear from her notify me immediately."

Hayden's tone was unusually calm for someone whose soul mate had just taken off. Of course, Serene assumed that he could contact Alaria whenever he pleased. Rounding on Serene, Hayden grinned.

"Well then, I suppose it's time we found you a room to stay in. Apparently there is a vacant slot in my bed, but I'm willing to bet that Alaria wouldn't accept that graciously. So, you're either bunking with Blaise or Damian." Hayden cocked an eyebrow at her, awaiting her answer.

"Blaise."

It wasn't Serene who answered. It was Damian. Crossing his arms over his chest, he fell silent once more, leaving no explanation to his response.

Blaise stood from his seat, a delighted grin crawling across his face. His eyes darted to Serene and he looked casually smug. She didn't have a choice about who she shared a bed with, but sleeping next to Blaise didn't pose any grounds for dispute.

Giving a perky smile, Serene stood. "Fine with me."

Across the room, Damian's eyes narrowed and he turned, stalking out of the room with an irritated grunt.

Paying little mind to Damian's actions, Hayden gave a pleased smile. "Well then, that's settled. Blaise, would you kindly show Serene around the house? I'll be my room if you need me."

Giving one last broad grin to Serene and Blaise, Hayden strode from the room, disappearing up a Brazilian Rosewood staircase.

In a split second, Serene could feel Blaise move considerably closer to her and she turned to him, an inch or so between their bodies.

Heat engulfed Serene's neck and face, her cheeks growing pink with flush. She gave a small nod and before she knew it, Blaise brushed his hand against hers, sending chills through her entire body. His skin was cold, almost like ice, but it soothed the heat caused by the blood pumping furiously through her veins. His fingers danced slowly up her arm before trailing back down to her fingers teasingly. Her heart skipped a beat, and she pressed her hand firmly against his as their fingers entwined, locking together.

Taking a deep breath, she looked to the side, a chaotic explosion rocketing through her mind. A day ago she had been with Ben and now, here she was, growing steadily closer to Blaise—a vampire. Dropping his hand hastily, she bit her lip.

"A-alright. I'm ready to see the house."

Blaise seemed slightly perturbed by her reluctance, his features screaming annoyance for a second, unnoticed by Serene. Quickly setting his expression back to content, he smiled down at her.

"Let's go."

Her initial view of the house wasn't entirely accurate. The rooms weren't all pitch black, as she had assumed. Many rooms were brightly lit; a welcoming sight for her. And, the house wasn't as filthy and abandoned as a first glance had led her to believe. A majority of the rooms were actually rather pleasant, filled with lavish furniture and decor from all over the world. Pieces of art centuries old hung gracefully on the walls, giving an insight to exactly how aged her new friends were.

The one room in the house that fit her previous assumptions was the kitchen. It was disheveled and clearly unused. The lights were completely turned off until Blaise switched them on to show her the room, several of the bulbs bursting at the sudden surge of energy they hadn't felt in ages. Cobwebs cluttered the corners and thick sheets of dust coated the floor.

"You can tell we eat out a lot," he joked, grinning.

Serene slapped on a wary smile, not exactly sure how to take his joke. Mustering her best grin, she followed him obediently throughout the remainder of the house.

Heading upstairs, Serene controlled her breathing as her heart began to race. The top of the landing turned into a lengthy hallway, doors on either side. Pacing past the numerous doors, Blaise played tour guide, telling her which room resided behind each wooden framed door.

"Damian's room is the third door to your left, the bathroom is the second door on your right, Hayden and Alaria's room is all the way down at the end," he explained, pointing to a door at the far end of the hallway, "and this," he stopped in front of a door that looked identical to the others, "is my room."

He turned the knob, pushed the door open slowly, and the two stepped inside.

CHAPTER 7

A large, king-sized bed was positioned against the far wall, a wooden table on either side, each occupied by an elegant lamp. The bed was elevated on a short platform, bringing it to just above waist height. Similar to the other rooms in the house, the windows were draped with curtains, preventing any light from straying in through the glass panes.

"Does sun kill you?"

This question had been on Serene's mind since the first time she had noticed the enclosed windows.

"It doesn't kill us, it just irritates our skin; like a strong sun burn." A playfully smile graced Blaise's lips. It seemed to Serene that he was a continually exultant person.

Skipping to the widow, Serene parted the curtains slowly, a small slit giving her just enough visibility to take in the surroundings outside without burning Blaise. However, it was beginning to rain, and the sun was buried behind a mass of gray clouds, looming over the manor like a bad omen.

The area around the house wasn't much to gape at. They were on the outskirts of Manchester, surrounded by other houses and a park or two. However, off in the distance, at the heart of the city, astounding towers rose from the ground, putting the old, uninteresting buildings surrounding them to shame. Hotels glistened through the mist, galleries and theaters adorning the marvelous city.

"Beautiful," breathed Serene, her eyes scanning the sight with amazement.

"Beautiful," Blaise repeated after her. However, his eyes lingered over her, rather than the scenery outside.

Turning and catching his gaze, Serene smiled self-consciously, tucking a stray lock of hair behind her ear.

In one swift motion, Blaise strode toward her, closing the length of the room between them. His movements were so immediate that Serene's eyes could hardly catch him.

She suddenly found herself with her back pressed firmly against the wall beside the window, Blaise pinning her by her wrists on either side of her neck. Breathing quickly, words stumbled through her brain, everything instantly incoherent. Blaise's eyes flashed a deep, lust filled blue, as he leaned down, his lips growing steadily closer to hers. In a teasing move, he shifted course, his cheek grazing coolly against hers, his lips parting slowly beside her ear.

"I never thought I'd feel so—intense—about my potential dinner," he breathed into her ear, his words practically hisses.

Biting her lip, Serene found herself breathless, her heart thrashing about madly in her chest, threatening to explode at any given moment. Uncertainty overtook her. She wanted to kiss him, to touch him, more than anything, but a small part of logic within her was screaming that something was wrong. Something about this entire situation was askew, out of place, and intensely dangerous.

His hand broke from her wrist and he set it lightly at the base of her neck, her veins pulsating beneath her skin, beneath his fingers, as he drew an invisible line up her neck and past her ear. His hand slid through her hair, her amber brown locks mingling between his grasp.

Hesitantly, Serene reached out, her fingertips grazing his cheek. His porcelain skin was cold, but not to the point of irritation. It was a soothing sensation that ensnared her senses and made her yearn for more.

His hand released itself from her hair, gliding sensually down her spine, bringing her body closer to his.

The door flew open with a sudden jolt, slamming against the wall with a shrieking bang. Damian stood in the doorway, his hidden gaze falling on the scene, but an angered expression already existent on his face that made Serene wonder if he had been spying on them.

Blaise rounded, his hands dropping quickly from Serene, leaving her dizzy headed and wobbling from the sudden rush of adrenaline.

"What is it Damian?" seethed Blaise, undoubtedly angered by the interruption.

Damian, seemingly pleased with himself for intruding when he did, relaxed his muscles, his expression easing as well.

"Hayden told me to take her out to eat. She is mortal, Blaise, and needs to eat more often than us."

Serene hadn't realized it until now, but her stomach was knotting up and gurgling with hunger. The mere prospect of food made her mouth water.

Blaise narrowed his gaze, but couldn't object to the raw facts. "Alright, I'll take her."

Damian's smirk widened. "You can't. Hayden needs your help contacting Alaria."

A deep growl formed in Blaise's throat, but he stifled it and strode from the room, evading Damian's grin as he went.

Serene remained motionless, not quite sure of what to do with herself. Thankfully, Damian didn't seem to want her opinion.

"Move."

It was one word, but the edge to his command was enough to make Serene jump slightly before hurrying out of the room, Damian at her heels all the way back down the hall, and the stairs, until they reached the front door where Serene paused for further instruction.

"What do you like to eat?" His voice was distant and impassive as he gazed down at her from behind his disheveled screen of hair.

"Um," Serene, too caught up in her interest in Damian, quickly racked her brain for an answer. "Anything is fine."

A small grunt was his only response as he pulled open the front door, nodding for Serene to go before him.

When she was clearly through the wooden frame and standing on the front steps, Damian stepped out, closing the door and glancing to the sky with a grateful expression. The clouds seemed to be hanging around, keeping the irritating glare of the sun at bay. Breathing in the crisp air, Damian walked down the stone steps, past Serene, and turned down the pathway. She followed quickly after, the rain, falling steadily now, clinging to her semi-wavy hair and slowly returning her hair to its curled state. Cursing softly under her breath, she wished she had her flat iron, but it was in the house somewhere, packed snugly in her pack, stuffed away in one of the numerous rooms.

Rounding the corner, just as Damian had done, a car came speeding backwards toward her. Jumping back and stumbling, she fell to the concrete pathway, instinctively setting her hands out to break her fall. Her skin made contact with the ground, roughly scratching against the sandpaper-like rock and peeling back bits of skin. Fresh blood oozed to the surface, leaving red trails across her palms.

The car came to a halt in front of her, the passenger's door swinging open toward her as Damian leaned out with a bemused smirk.

"Get in."

"Yeah, I'm fine. Thanks for asking," she hissed, her voice laced with sarcasm.

Standing and brushing her hands off on her jeans, she cringed as pain shot through her open wounds. Sliding into the passenger's seat and closing the door, she threw on her seat belt and examined her lacerations.

"Clumsy?" came Damian's mocking voice from beside her as he backed quickly out of the driveway, not bothering glancing at her. His nose twitched at the scent of fresh blood.

"Not usually."

"Maybe next time I'll hit you and see if we can't get those reflexes up to par." A barely noticeable smile twitched at the corners of his lips.

The remainder of the ride was quiet as they sped through the winding streets of Manchester, heading toward the center of the city. Houses whirled by like blurs, giving Serene the distinct feeling that they were traveling at a speed well above the limit. The fascination between men, cars, and driving fast eluded her and she rolled her eyes at the speed gauge, the needle steadily climbing higher.

Rounding a sharp turn, the road stretched out in a seemingly endless expanse of asphalt, dozens of shops and restaurant's peppering each side. Every now and then the heavenly scent of a cheeseburger would waft through an open door, dancing through the open car window and teasing Serene's nose. A low growl echoed from her stomach, causing her to grasp at her torso in aggravation.

"Pick a place." Damian's eyes jumped from the right side of the street to the left, staring down all of the possible places to stop.

There were dozens of restaurants to choose from, making it all the more difficult to decide. Serene's stomach continued to knot itself up and she feared that it might just start to digest itself if she didn't eat something soon.

"There," she muttered, pointing to a small sandwich shop on the right side of the street, several smaller shops flanking it on either side.

Swiftly, Damian parked the car, nearly hitting three others in the process, but expertly evading each of them. Before Serene could even undo her seatbelt, Damian was out of the car, waiting by the restaurant door, an impatient frown plastered across his jaw.

Taking her time, she unfastened her seatbelt, checked her reflection in the mirror—three times—and finally, as leisurely as possible, she stepped out of the car, striding over to Damian. His expression had quickly gone from impatient to genuinely irritated, his lips curving into a sneer as Serene gave him a cheeky grin.

"We're getting food and getting out. I need to stop some-where before we go back to the house."

Nodding, Serene slipped into the restaurant, closely fol-lowed by Damian, his watchful eyes never letting her out of his sight.

Emerging half an hour later, Damian breathed deeply, replacing the strong stench of cheeseburgers with the linger-ing smell of blood, coursing through hundreds of bodies, wandering here and there, some mere inches from him.

Serene appeared slightly after him, content with her filled stomach. Damian's sour attitude toward her was beginning to grow old. Was it simply because she was human that made him so icy, or was there something else, something far deeper that she wouldn't understand even if he explained it? What-ever the case, it was concerning and annoying, leaving Serene to wonder constantly about him and his thoughts.

Eager to get to their next stop and get home, she wasted no time, managing to beat him to the car and buckle up before he was even halfway across the sidewalk. It seemed to her that he was the one biding his time now. Walking around the car and glancing for traffic, he pulled open his door, clambering in and situating himself.

"Where's the fire?" he asked, intrigue definite in his tone.

"I just want to get home to—get some sleep." Truthfully, she was eager to see Blaise. Eager to sleep next to Blaise.

"I'm sure," he muttered, his sour expression returning as he shifted the car into drive and pulled away from the curb. It took Serene a moment to notice that he was traveling five miles *below* the speed limit. Raising an eyebrow, she looked over at him, but his eyes were intensely set on the road. Suddenly, it seemed like Damian had all the time in the world.

Well, technically, he did.

About five minutes down the road, they pulled over again and, as Serene had predicted, Damian took his time vacating the vehicle. She beat him to the door of the shop, glancing it over as she waited.

It was a small book store with novels and biographies cluttering the front windows. A small, black sign hung on the door, reading 'OPEN' with several weekdays and times below it in smaller, white lettering.

Peering through the pane of glass embedded in the door, Serene could make out a few shadowy figures retreating down the long isles of books, their heads turning from side to side as they scanned the titles. Damian meandered up from behind her, brushing past her and into the shop, quickly grasping her wrist and pulling her in.

The shop was even gloomier inside than it had appeared outside. The lighting was horrid, and a thick cloud of dust wafted through the air, tickling Serene's nose. Sneezing, she covered her mouth with her sleeve, trying to filter the grimy air. Breathing through the cotton fabric of her sleeve was like trying to suck air through a straw—damn near impossible. Finally, she gave up and took a large gasp of the disgusting air, coughing and sputtering as she did so. How the rest of the shoppers could stand it was beyond her.

Looking around, she realized that there were only three other people in the entire shop, or at least that she could see. The customer furthest down the isles was decked in black, looking perfectly at home in the obscurity. The second customer, however, was a tall blonde, adorned in a pink sweater and jean skirt, pumps adding at least two inches to her height. Mixed in with the decaying books and morbid shopper, she looked like a Barbie doll stuck in the middle of an occult gathering.

The cashier was so gloomy she practically blended into the wall.

"Stay here," came Damian's voice from beside Serene as he watched her intently, his eye like daggers, a wordless threat. With one last glance, he disappeared down the strip of books, meeting with a shadowy figure at the end of the isle and disappearing into a back room.

Instantly, Serene's mind swarmed. Now was her chance to escape.

If she had any hope of making it out of this, she'd have to leave. Now. Something inside her wanted to stay, wanted to get to know Damian, Hayden, and especially Blaise, but her rational thinking kicked in, intensifying the situation.

Peering down the murky isle, she strained her eyes, willing them to pick up shadows in the distance. Seeing no one, her mind shifted to the shoppers. Would they rat her out? Looking down the other isles, her gaze located Barbie, but not the other. Barbie wouldn't notice her existence-or lack there of, even if she ran around screaming at the top of her lungs.

Time was, once again, creeping in on Serene, forcing her to make a decision that could potentially change her life forever. She wanted so badly to wait it out and see what happened, specifically between she and Blaise, but the fear of dying led her down the path of the latter choice; running.

Silently, and without further hesitation, she turned and walked casually toward the door, not daring to make any rash movements that might draw attention to herself. As she reached the shop door, she pushed it open slowly and stepped out into the damp air.

The rain had stopped, but puddles still remained on the sidewalk and roads. Closing the door soundlessly behind her, she turned, took a few steps, and broke into a mad dash. She knew that she had to put as much distance between herself and Damian in as little time as possible, otherwise he'd pick up her scent.

She needed to find a crowd—and fast.

CHAPTER 8

Puddles splashed up around her ankles as she darted down the sidewalk, weaving in and out of the many pedestrians, their eyes zoning in on her in confusion. Even on the crowded shopping strip, Serene knew that Damian could pick up her scent. Her only hope was to leave a false trail and hide out elsewhere. Dodging taxis, she dashed across the street, ignoring the slander being screamed at her from taxi drivers, forced to stop abruptly. Scanning the vicinity, a large crowd could be seen gathering a few blocks away. Whatever they were looking at was beyond her, but she knew that the crowd was her best option—her only option.

Emerging from the back room, a slip of paper grasped in his hand, Damian's eyes narrowed. His nose twitched in the air for a split second and his eyes suddenly flashed a dangerous shade of dark violet. He knew, even before reaching the front of the store, that she was gone. Her scent no longer thickened the air. All that remained was the familiar smell of dust that coated the book store.

Quickly, Damian, letting out a low growl, rushed from the store, sprinting down the sidewalk, gracefully maneuvering between the shoppers. He could smell Serene, knew she had come this way, but couldn't see her anywhere. Hayden would kill him if he lost track of her—if he disobeyed orders. Letting her go wasn't an option. With these thoughts clicking through his mind, he picked up speed, moving like a flash down the sidewalk.

Reaching the crowd, Serene found them all gathered around a gangly looking man, picking away on his guitar; a hat sat by his feet, slowly filling to the brim with coins and crinkled bills. Her heart was thumping away in her chest, anxiety growing as seconds ticked by. Damian would find her in a heartbeat if she didn't keep moving. Quickly, she scanned the crowd as if looking for somebody in particular.

A devious smirk twitched on Damian's lips. For a few moments, he had begun to believe that she had gotten away, but a deep breath filled his lungs with her fragrance.

Eyes narrowing to slits, his gaze fell on a small gathering a few stores away. Stealthily, he walked down the street, reached the edge of the crowd and blended in quickly, alert of every blood pulsing body around him. With one quick look over, he spotted her; her long brown hair hanging down onto her jacket, back turned to him, and sticking out like a sore thumb.

As quickly and quietly as he could, he lurked in and out of the winding bodies, never lifting his eyes from his unseeing prey. Inches from her, he drew a deep breath, her scent radiating from her and seeping through his nose. Abruptly, he lunged, his hand latching onto her shoulder firmly, a mocking grin being released across his face. With a sharp jerk, he spun her around, prepared to carry her back to the house if she went easily, or kill her then and there if she resisted. As she whipped around, a look of fright flashed through her eyes, met by the astounded expression on Damian's face.

It wasn't Serene.

The girl held firmly in his grasp struggled against him, threatening to scream before he released her.

"That sneak!"

Recognition washed over him like a sickening illness. Serene had tricked him, giving her jacket to some random look-alike, her scent sticking to the synthetic fabrics, leading him on a false trail. She could be anywhere by now.

Glaring, he hissed as the rain started up again, washing away any trail she might have left behind. Damian glanced around once more, considering letting her go.

An alley stretched into the darkness in front of Serene, giving her the unnerving feeling that something sinister might be looming at the other end, but it was her only escape route. Slinking into the shadows of the alley, she held her breath, training her ears to the silence, hoping to pick up the sounds of even the stealthiest of attackers.

She didn't know Damian—didn't know how long he'd bother searching; if he'd call in Hayden and Blaise. Her only hope was to hide out for as long as she could, using the rain to mask her scent and keep her undetected.

The shadows of the alley were comforting in a way; like a blanket, shielding her from the dangers of the world she found herself in. Rain fell like iced bullets, blurring the edges of the world around her and confusing her senses.

Was that footsteps she heard, or rain drops against the cement?

Brick walls rose to the sky on either side of her, windowless and bleak. Night was quickly descending, taking away what little light the sun had managed to shine through the clouds before and replacing it with the soft, luminous glow of the moon.

Slivers of moonlight bounced off the puddles, giving Serene just enough glow to see about a foot in front of her. A dead silence had followed her down the alley; the soft strumming of the guitar player no longer humming in her ears. Part of her now regretted ever running. At least with Damian she would have had a place to stay at night, rather than trudging down dark alleys in the rain. But she knew that staying with a gathering of vampires was a death sentence.

Slowing her pace halfway down the alley and sighing, her shoe caught on the edge of a rock. Stumbling, she caught herself on the brick wall and a low snicker echoed distinctly, not too far away.

Heart in her throat, Serene froze. Perhaps it was the rain tricking her again. 'It's nothing. Just the rain.', she thought to herself. Her assumptions were quickly proven false as a definite shadow stirred in the obscurity, rocks kicking up from the concrete walk.

"Didn't your mother ever tell you to steer clear of dark alleys?" came an unfamiliar voice, a slight tone of amusement laced through the shadow's tone.

Serene treaded backwards quickly, putting distance between herself and the approaching shadow. A tall, pale boy appeared, gazing intently at her through the beams of moonlight. His hair was an alarming shade of blue; his eyes practically black. Being not much taller than Serene, she wouldn't have found him to be much of a threat, but the two, piercing fangs shining in the moonlight changed things.

A scream began to form in Serene's throat, but just as she was about to release it, she found an icy hand smothering her mouth. With a sharp tug, she was pulled backwards, her body pressing up against whoever was silencing her. Before she could grasp what was occurring, sudden motion from behind the blue haired boy caught her eye.

Two more shadows were emerging from the depth of the alley, smirking at the sight of their friend's captured prey. Serene could only assume that whoever was now holding tightly to her was with them. She wasn't just facing one vampire now; she was facing four—none of which were her new found "friends."

The newcomers were both male, each sporting their own vibrant hair color. On the right stood a boy with a vicious grin, his hair a violent red. He was taller than the others as far as she could see, not able to get a look at the one holding her. On the left, a mop of shimmering violet cascaded over the shortest boy's eyes, his expression vacant and blithe.

"Looks like you've caught us a nice little snack, Stephen," said the red haired vampire to the blue haired one, who was slowly inching toward her, streaks of moonlight ricocheting wildly off of him.

"It appears that way, Marcus," Stephen muttered without looking back.

"She looks a bit meager to me," came the third boy, leaning against the alley wall, unamused, not a flicker of emotion crossing his features.

"Then you can find your own snack, Luke," replied Stephen. His arrogance toward the others set him apart as the leader of the pack.

Her captor, his hand still clasped tightly over her mouth, remained unseen and unheard. His body shifted behind hers and he released her, thrusting her toward Stephen with intense force. Hands latched onto her, gripping at her forearms and torso, Stephen, Marcus, and Luke all grasping out at her at once. Serene screamed, kicked and punched, trying to push them from her. Managing to turn her back to them, her eyes landed on the fourth.

Gawking, her eyes flashed up and down the boy. Tan and brawny, he differed from the others. His eyes lacked the blood thirsty look that the trio held and he shivered against the rain. It was almost as if—

He was human. The fourth boy wasn't a vampire at all; he was a human.

A perplexed and almost troubled aura fell over Serene like a wool blanket. Why would he do this? Why would a human help such monsters in the capture of an innocent girl? It didn't make any sense to her, but there was no time to mull it over. Time, as usual, was not on her side.

Preparing to cry out for help, she took a sudden and sharp intake of air only to have it knocked out of her as she was slammed to the ground.

A fifth figure had arrived, seemingly falling from the roof of the buildings surrounding the alley and landing next to her, pushing her to the concrete forcefully. Through the shadows, she could barely make out was going on, but had a strong notion not to get up. Shielding her head with her hands, she flinched as legs slammed into her accidentally. A brawl was taking place around her, the fifth figure apparently not pleased with the group's actions. Hisses were emitted sporadically and curse words were strewn throughout the grunts and moans of the ongoing battle.

Kicked to the side, Serene's arms scraped against the stony cement, leaving trails of blood up and down her skin, the copper smell of the red liquid polluting the air. Quickly, she tried to burry her scratched arms beneath her chest, but it was too late. The scent of blood had immediately soaked the air and the crimson liquid was now dripping into the puddles encircling her.

The surrounding chaos froze abruptly and Serene could feel five pairs of eyes gazing down at her. In a heartbeat, two bodies dove at her, their hands clawing at her, tearing her shirt and matting up her hair. Her screaming echoed through the alley and, with a sudden roar, the two were pulled away from her and slammed effortlessly against the alley walls. The fifth figure yanked her from the ground and slung her over his shoulder.

Quickly, and without looking back at the scene, he sprinted from the alley, emerging on the now empty sidewalk, his breathing rushed, as if angry. Serene, upside down, couldn't make out which way was up and which way was down. Disoriented and confused, she hung limp over her savior's shoulder, glad to be out of that mess. Her body was cut up nicely; her arms especially, blood still seeping from her cuts. A bruise or two had even begun to form on her forearms.

She heard a door open and, spinning upright, found herself situated in the front seat of a car, the door closing beside her quickly. Without a second to think, the driver's door swung open and words gushed from Serene's mouth.

"Help! I've been kidnaped by Vampi—"

Her words were cut short.

Damian's irate eyes peered out at her, his veil of black hair strewn across his forehead.

CHAPTER 9

A white blur flew toward her, slamming her head against the car window, Damian's hand clenched around her throat.

"What didn't you understand about not running?" he hissed through gritted teeth, his grasp loosening, making sure not to hurt her.

Struggling against his weight, she narrowed her eyes to a glare, locking in on him like a sniper targeting her prey. Balling her hands up into fists, she took a deep breath and sent a right hook speeding toward his face.

Reacting quicker than she had expected, his palm stopped her punch, his fingers encasing her hand like a claw in one of those arcade games that no one can ever seem to win. Pain shot through her fingers, crawling through her bones before he let go, an apologetic smile twitching at the corners of his lips. Shaking his hair into his eyes quickly, he slouched into his seat, dead eyeing the road.

"Sorry."

Serene, shaking with mixed emotions, watched Damian closely. What made him so different from the others? So apologetic and caring? Why was it that he, who showered her with icy stares and snide remarks, radiated a sense of protection? It didn't make sense.

The ride back to the house was excruciating. Before even pulling away, Damian had activated the power door locks, cutting off the only escape route available. Of course, escaping never once crossed Serene's mind from inside the car. Only a mad man would try their luck at fleeing, with Damian sitting right there; not to mention the fact that she'd have to jump from a car that was currently speeding at well over eighty miles per hour, barely cutting sharp turns.

Hayden would kill her for this. And if he didn't, when Alaria heard she sure would. No matter how she sliced the situation, Serene always found her fate to be one thing; death. If only the vampires back in the alley had finished her off; she wouldn't have to face this.

The car came to a shuddering halt. They were home. Why couldn't Damian have chosen now to be slow? Now, when her life was moments from ending? Caught in her whirlwind of thoughts, she hadn't noticed Damian exit the car. Before she knew it, he was at her side, pulling her gently from the passenger seat and steering her up the stony path to the house.

She could feel his eyes burning into her back, watching her every move. She tried dragging her feet; tried stumbling over stones; she even tried bending down to tie her shoe, anything to hinder her arrival, knowing that once inside she'd never leave again.

Fear was slowly choking her, her heart rate picking up, her fingers shaking. Every step she took toward the house intensified her panic, and she considered running for a brief instant. Her moment of insanity passed and she was soon staring blankly at the wooden door that, not too long ago, had seemed almost enchanting. Now it seemed oppressing; a mark of the death to come. An icy void lingered behind her, Damian's shadow crawling up the frame of the door as he pressed in from behind, his arm reaching past her to the doorknob. With one graceful push, the door swung on hinge, revealing the dimly lit living room.

Pushed through the door, Serene gulped. Hayden and Blaise both sat perched on the edge of their seats, tense expressions clouding their features. As if a bomb had gone off, they lunged from their perches, practically levitating across the floor to where Serene and Damian now stood. Thankfully, their piercing eyes fell on Damian, saving her from the burning intensity.

"Where have you been?" boomed Hayden, a look of fury washing over him. "How long can it possibly take to get her something to eat? You've been gone for well over three hours." His words were like venom dripping from his fangs.

Serene stared intently at the floor. If Hayden was this infuriated about them being late she didn't want to stick around and find out how he would react when he learned of what she had done. Slowly, she began to inch backwards, but before she could take three steps, Damian's hand was secured on her shoulder.

Blaise's eyes held her in his view, raising an eyebrow and scowling slightly before looking back to Damian. "We thought you'd eaten her or something." His tone came out lighter than Hayden's; almost mockingly. Damian's brow furrowed.

"We had to make a few stops on the way home. I went to the book store."

Suddenly, the anger seemed to be sucked right out of the room by Damian's words. The edges of Hayden's mouth turned up into a grin, a look of complete understanding glinting in his eyes.

"Very well, Damian. Blaise, take Serene to your room. It's late and she needs sleep."

It was over before it ever began. The insurmountable fear that had been slowly engulfing Serene since being captured by Damian was suddenly leaking from her, all sense or horror gone. Damian hadn't told the others of her attempted escape.

As Blaise tugged her away, she glanced over her shoulder, her eyes watching Damian carefully for any sign of betrayal still glimmering in his eyes. Of course, his eyes were, as usual, hidden beneath his hair, but she could tell by his relaxed stance that he wasn't going to snitch. Emitting a sigh of relief, she clambered up the stairs ahead of Blaise, turning down the wall and straight to his room, hesitating outside the door.

"You don't have to wait to go in. It's as much my room as it is yours while you're here." Something in his tone led her to believe that she'd be there for quite some time—with or without her consent. That thought aside, she pushed the door open, entering the room for the second time that day.

It hadn't changed. The bed still sat centered against the wall. It struck Serene as slightly unorthodox that there wasn't a second bed set up for her.

However, she wasn't complaining. Sharing a bed with Blaise was hardly a concern. Looking the room over once more, she noticed that there was a small difference. Her pajamas had been set out nicely on the end of the bed; blue shorts and a white tank top. Blaise took a moment to open the closet, revealing the remainder of her belongings, hung gently on hangers. Her suitcase sat on the closet floor, her cosmetics and whatnot still inside.

Muffling a yawn, Serene sat down on the edge of the bed, grasping her pajamas lazily. Shifting her eyes to Blaise, she wondered if he'd leave the room while she changed.

"Um … could I have a moment to change?" Her question came out weakly.

Without a word, Blaise turned his back to her, staring attentively at the wall, a devious smirk playing across his lips.

It wasn't exactly the type of privacy Serene had been counting on, but she didn't dare kick Blaise out of his own room. Tentatively, she rose from the foot of the bed, pacing to the opposite end of the room from him and turning her back to his. Kicking off her shoes, she peeled over her socks, kicking them to the corner. Quickly, glancing over her shoulder now and then to make sure he wasn't peeking, she slid off her grimy jeans and t-shirt and pulled on her tank top and shorts, pleased to have clean clothes clinging to her body. A wave of fatigue was washing over her. She'd have to take a shower in the morning.

Pulling her hair free from the entrapment of her collar, it tumbled down her back. Pivoting, she looked to Blaise, her eyes focused on the back of his head. And, as if he could feel her stare, he turned, smiling. Without an ounce of hesitation, he pulled his shirt up over his head, dropping it to the floor gracefully. Having some sense of decency and acknowledgment of Serene's shyness, he left his jeans on and walked to the bed, sliding beneath the covers with one swift motion.

Serene stood by her side of the bed, a forced smile evident on her face. The only person Serene had ever been physically

close with was Ben. And even with him, she had never shared
a bed.

"Don't worry. I won't bite." His smile captivated her, seemingly drawing her into the bed, and she let out a small laugh.
How ironically funny.

Sliding beneath the covers, she kept her distance from him,
keeping a good foot or so between their bodies. It was slowly
donning on her how immensely dangerous falling asleep next
to a vampire might actually be. Sleep no longer seemed to be a
pressing matter although her eyes stung from being awake so
long.

Questions flooded Serene's mind as she shifted to her side,
looking to Blaise who tilted his head to meet her gaze.

"Blaise.." she began, trailing off.

"Yes?"

"What's it like? I mean, being what you are."

"It's," he paused for a moment, his brow furrowing pensively, "relaxing. Time isn't an issue for me like it is for
humans. I'll live forever."

"Doesn't that bother you?"

He gave a grave smile. "Not so much. It gives me a chance
to meet so many interesting people." His eyes searched hers
carefully.

Serene nodded, gears in her head working furiously.

"I still don't understand how you can resist, well, killing
me. All of the movies and books I've seen and read made it
sound like vampires were all killing machines without souls."

He laughed, shaking the bed. "That's Hollywood for you.
Eating for me is just like eating for you. Yes, blood is
immensely tempting, more than you can imagine, but I've
dealt with this for years. It's like an addiction; once you've

mastered control over it, it no longer consumes your life. I was once like those vampires you see in movies; ravenous and beastly, but I've been around long enough to control that."

A cringe shook through Serene at the thought of him once being a monster. Well, more-so than he was now.

"Today, with Damian, we stopped at some book store. He went into the back. What was that all about?"

A dark look seemed to cloud Blaise's features for a second. Had she said too much? Seen too much? His eyes hazed, as if he were searching for an appropriate response.

"Like drug addicts, we have a dealer," he furrowed his brow, "Sort of anyway. There are humans out there that work for vampires; helping them survive."

Serene's mind flashed to the boy in the alley.

"There is a supplier at the book store that keeps a list of known criminals in the area. We pay him to supply us with names. It makes it easier to find the bad guys to make sure we don't accidentally kill someone that's harmless."

That made sense, but she had a feeling that she wasn't getting the entire story. It boggled her mind that, in the tiny back room of that innocent book store, a behind the scenes operation was being run. A service providing victims for vampires.

"That's funny. I don't recall learning about Vampire Blood Banks in health class."

He smirked. "Well, I'd hope not. We try our best to go undetected. That's mainly why everyone is so uptight about you being here. If you escape and word gets out about our existence," his words faded, a grim expression replacing his smile. "It'll be like the Salem Witch hunts for vampires."

"But I won't try—"

"To escape? But you already have."

Her jaw dropped. "How did you know?"

"Damian. He was so close to you—so guarded, almost as if he was protecting you from something. He's never been that way before. Not since—" his words broke off.

"Since what?"

"Well, not for a long time. He's usually very distant from others, especially humans. When I saw him so watchful of you I knew that something must have happened while you were out."

Biting her lip, Serene looked mortified. Was Blaise angry? Would he tell Hayden? As if reading her expression, he chuckled.

"Don't worry. Your secret's safe with me, but I'd prefer you didn't leave."

Her expression mingled between confused and threatened. "Why?"

"Because," a dazzling smile broke out across his face as he leaned into her. "I'd miss you too much."

Left in complete awe by his sudden closeness and charming words, she blinked, gathering her muddled thoughts.

"Now, shouldn't you get some sleep? You look exhausted."

As he leaned back to his pillow, her head seemed to clear.

"What about you? Aren't you going to sleep? And why don't you sleep during the day instead of the night?"

"I don't need as much sleep as you do. I can run on one night's sleep for three or four days without any exhaustion. And we try to blend in as much as possible with the humans. It wouldn't look very natural if I only came out at night, now would it?" A teasing smile played on his lips. "Besides, it's generally rainy here most of the time; makes for nice cloud coverage during the day."

Nodding, she set her head on her pillow, her eyes never leaving him. As he reached over to the bedside table and turned out his light, the room was engulfed by shadows and the overwhelming sensation to move closer to him bubbled up inside Serene. Suppressing it, she turned to her stomach, setting her face in her pillow.

Drifting in between consciousness and sleep, Serene could feel Blaise's eyes watching her through the darkness.

Morning came, but no sunlight penetrated the dark shades to awaken Serene. Her alarm for this morning was the slamming of a door somewhere down the hall. Nearly having a heart attack, her eyes snapped open, fear crippling her for a moment as she oriented herself.

Angry whispers penetrated the door, ringing in her ears. Looking over, she found Blaise missing, his side of the bed neatly made as if he'd never been in it. Shifting the covers off of her body, heat poured out in a puff. She hadn't realized it before, but the room was stifling hot without Blaise's icy presence to balance it out. Her shorts stuck to her legs as she crawled out of bed, tiptoeing to the door.

The closer she grew to the door, the more pronounced the whispers became. Reaching the door, she pressed her ear up against it, straining to hear what was being said.

"You're lucky she didn't get away," came Blaise's voice in a chilling hiss.

"She's here isn't she? That's all that matters." Damian retorted.

"If Hayden found out about this—"

The voice trailed off as if Blaise had picked up her presence. Several inaudible mutters followed before footsteps announced the coming of one and the going of the other. The identities of the coming and going were beyond her. Quickly retreating backwards, she scuttled to the closet.

Serene was pretending to pick out an outfit for the day as the door swung open, Blaise entering without so much as a knock. Looking over her shoulder, Serene gave a mocking gasp.

"I could have been naked!" Her eyes narrowed into a teasing glare.

"I'm not that lucky."

Pursing her lips together with distaste, she aimlessly grabbed a fresh change of clothes from the closet and turned, rolling her eyes at him as he stared on smugly.

"I'm going to get a shower."

"I suppose it would be rude if I asked to tag along?"

His words sent blush rocketing through her cheeks and she quickly slipped out of the room and down the hall, somewhat pleased to leave the awkward conversation behind her. Apparently, sharing a bed for one night gave Blaise the notion that he could make as many sexual innuendos as he pleased.

The bathroom, though small, was comforting in a homey way. The walls were a warm shade of off-white and a plush, black rug was sprawled out carelessly on the floor, waiting eagerly to catch stray drops of water as patrons stepped out of the shower. Closing the door and locking it, Serene set her clothing down on the marble top that surrounded the sink. Glancing to the mirror, she looked herself over.

Disheveled described her state nicely. Her hair was knotted at the ends, giving her a bed head look—and not a sexy one. The rain and dirt from last night had left a brown smudge or two on her elbows; her hands were another story all together.

Grimacing, she started the shower, waiting impatiently as the heat adjusted while she scrambled out of her pajamas, peeling them from her body.

When the water had reached a reasonable degree of heat, not scolding but just about, she stepped over the rim of the tub and into the shower, standing as directly under the pulsating water as she could. Breathing in the steam, the water engulfed her body, washing away the dirt and grim of yesterday along with any fears that still lingered within her.

A thousand thoughts were jumbled together in one messy pile building up in her mind. Just a few days ago she had been considering her future, Ben being the center point. Now, she was being held captive in a house of vampires, thoughts of Ben gone from her mind. It was as if she was an entirely different person. But this was what she had come to England looking for, right? A new Serene? The real Serene? Vampires and bottled up lust hadn't been part of the plan. Until now.

Her feelings for Blaise were complex. Part of her, the sensible, old Serene, warned her to stay away, to try and escape. Nothing good could come from this situation. But another part of her, the new part, told her to live in the moment. What was the worst that could happen?

I could be sucked dry, she thought pessimistically.

And then there was the fear factor. Blaise seemed harmless enough, and Hayden seemed more than welcoming, but that left Alaria and Damian. Alaria had turned her nose up at the mere sight of Serene, even putting forth as much hate driven effort to flee the country. Damian, on the other hand, was harshly protective in a way that left Serene wondering if he wanted to hurt her or was trying to save her. Whatever the case, she felt perfectly safe at the moment, feeling practically at home in the warmth of the shower.

When her skin had been washed raw, turning bright red, and her hair squeaked between her fingers, not a trace of dirt left, she turned off the water and stepped out onto the rug. A shiver ran the course of her body as the cold air in the bathroom mingled with the fresh water droplets on her skin, creating an arctic breeze effect.

Folding her arms in a feeble attempt at keeping warm, she looked around in horror. In her hurry to escape Blaise's relentless stare she had forgotten a towel. Straying out into the hallway, naked, in a house filled with men didn't seem appealing, but neither did standing exposed to the harsh chill of the bathroom. *Great, Serene. Just great.*

"Forget something?" breathed a voice from behind the bathroom door. She recognized it as Hayden. What was with these guys and appearing out of nowhere? Were they spying on her?

"Um, yeah. I forgot to grab a towel."

"I'll leave one at the base of the door for you."

Before she could answer, a small shadow dropped to the floor just on the other side of the bathroom door and Hayden's footsteps disappeared down the stairs.

Timidly, Serene padded over to the door and unlocked it, listening intently for the stealthy footsteps of a person walking down the hall. After a moment of dead silence, she cautiously opened the door. The towel was folded squarely and sat just in front of her. Quickly, she bent down and grabbed it, scooping it up and closing the door.

The soft cotton of the towel against her body was an inviting feeling after standing against the icy air for several minutes. After carefully drying off, being sure not to leave a drop of water behind, she grabbed her clothes from the counter and hastily pulled them on. Using the towel to ring her hair out, she glared as her auburn strands fell down her back in loose curls. How annoying. Trying to run her fingers through her hair to straighten the strands, she found her effort futile as the curls bounded back into place. A look of chagrin dominated her features.

Without her makeup bag or flat iron, which she had left in her suitcase, she found her bathroom time cut in half. Hanging her towel on a hook on the wall, she departed from the bathroom, not quite sure what to do with herself at this point. When were they going to let her go?

There was no doubt in her mind that her mother would have sent out the National Guard by now to search for her missing daughter. Hayden and the others couldn't plan on holding her captive too much longer, could they? Although, part of Serene wanted to stay—if only for Blaise.

Quickly, silently, she stepped out into the hallway, looking down each end with wary eyes. Heading back in the direction of Blaise's room, she paused by the door, her eyes flickering for just a second to see if he was still there. He wasn't, and that slightly unnerved her. If he wasn't there then where was he? Turning her head, her gaze fell on Hayden's door at the very end of the hall. It became apparent to Serene that Blaise had steered clear of Hayden's room, not even bothering taking her any further down the hall than to the room she'd be staying in. Biting her lip, she cautiously proceeded, finishing off the length of the hall until she reached Hayden's door. Knocking crossed her mind, but further examination brought it to her attention that the door stood ajar, practically welcoming her inside. Curiosity killed the cat, not a vampire; she'd be fine.

Hayden's room was bigger than Blaise's, and much more lavish. Of course, he did come off as the leader of the house hold, despite the fact that he wasn't much older than Blaise and Damian, at least not in appearance anyway. Alaria's presence clearly altered aspects of the room, adding a feminine touch amongst the manliness.

Amidst a cluttered collection of odds and ends stood a small, crystal vase with a few wilting roses; clearly Hayden lacked a green thumb. The roses were only a small price to pay for the absence of Alaria. She wouldn't be missed; not by Serene at any rate.

The bed wasn't much bigger than Blaise's, but she was sure that sleeping alone in it would make anyone feel awfully lonely. An aura of mystery clung to the room, as if there were some reason she shouldn't be there. Then again, she *shouldn't* be in the house in general. She should be at home. Advancing deeper into the room, her eyes glanced around rapidly, taking in as much as she could before her nerves got the best of her.

Approaching the right side of the bed, a glimmer caught her eye from within the bedside table drawer which was partially open. The light in the room seemed to be shining down and bouncing off of some glossy piece of paper. Looking down toward the table, she paced toward it, arm outstretched toward the drawer.

Her hand made contact with something that was not the drawer. Suddenly, without any warning what-so-ever, some-one had stepped in front of her and was now defiantly block-ing her path. Tilting her head up, her eyes traveled the length of a figure, their arms crossed in a guarding manner across their muscular chest.

Eyebrows raised and questioning eyes, Hayden stared down at her, standing tall and firm before her short and feeble stance.

"Looking for something?"

CHAPTER 10

His eyes burned into her, curiosity and irritation distinctly scripted in his features. Taking an impetuous step back, she shook her head.

"No. I'm sorry. The door was open and I—"

"Just because a door is open doesn't imply a invitation to enter," he stated casually, his vigilant stance never faltering. With one swift motion he turned Serene around on her heels and ushered her from the room. Once in the hallway, Hayden closed the door and looked down at Serene with an authoritative stare.

"I must ask you not to enter my room again, Serene. While this may not be your home, I would hope you'd respect my privacy."

Nodding swiftly, she muttered an apology under her breath and was herded further down the hall, back to Blaise's room, where she found Blaise waiting patiently on the bed, flipping through a magazine that was torn and faded; centuries old. His eyes trailed up from the withering magazine and a smile crossed his face.

"I was beginning to think you had drowned in the shower."

"I was looking for..," Serene glanced over her shoulder, but Hayden was gone. Furrowing her brow, puzzled, she looked back to Blaise. "I'm fine."

In awareness of her statement, he nodded and set the magazine aside, rising from his seated position on the bed.

"Today will be fun," he promised, smirking as he walked toward her.

"What are we going to do?"

"We're going to—"

A loud bang from the story below cut off his sentence, bringing his attention to the bedroom door as Damian slammed through, anger dominating his visible scowl.

"We've got visitors," he breathed through clenched teeth with seemingly forced effort.

"What? Why?" Blaise shifted, shielding Serene from the door and any possible attackers that might find their way upstairs.

"*Her.*"

"Serene? What would they want with her?" A low growl built up behind Blaise's words.

"They know she's here. They know she knows our secret and they don't trust her." His eyes were hidden behind his hair, but Serene was sure they were narrowed into a piercing glare. "This is all my fault." His last words were barely audible to Serene and made no sense, but she didn't have time to think it over.

Blaise linked his arm around her waist and pulled her from the room, her feet barely grazing the floor.

"Stay close to me," he hissed, descending the stairs to discover the scene unfolding.

Setting Serene on her feet, she stared on in horror. Hayden was fending off three male vampires on his own. A chill ran down her spine as she narrowed her eyes. She knew these vampires; Stephen, Marcus, and Luke. Her assassins from the alley. After realizing that Damian was a vampire and had rescued her, they must have deciphered that she'd been running from him. But how did they know where to find her? Something didn't add up.

Flinching, she watched the fight ensue. It was three against three; a fair fight. Her eyes flickered madly between the pairs fighting for her. Hayden had gone up against Stephen, Blaise took on Marcus, and Damian was hurling blurred punches at Luke. Everything was so fast paced that Serene could hardly keep up. A floorboard creaked from behind her and she rounded quickly. A tall, muscular, male figure towered over her, encasing her in his arms and pulling her up the stairs quickly.

They moved at human pace down the hall before he flung her into Blaise's room, slamming the door. Before she could scream, the figure clasped a hand over her mouth. Frantically struggling to contain her, he sat her on the edge of the bed, kneeling to bring himself to eye level with her. It was the boy from the alley; the one that had held her captive once before. His eyes, however, were not threatening, but rather sympathetic and his actions hurried. With a look that calmed her, he began to speak.

"I shouldn't be doing this, but you have to know. These people—these vampires, they—" Thundering footsteps were charging up the staircase and a frantic look flashed through the boy's eyes. "Don't trust anyone." Releasing her, he stood quickly and made a mad dash for the window, pausing to glance at her.

"What's your name?" Serene asked, her words slurring as she rushed.

"Dean."

Before she could ask anything else, he was gone, disappearing out the window and down the brick siding, leaving her dazed.

Blaise barged through the bedroom door, a trail of blood inching down his cheek from his forehead.

"Are you alright? How did you get up here? Was there another one? Did he hurt you?" Releasing the Spanish Inquisition on her, Serene hardly had time to think her answers through.

"I'm fine. I-ran up here to hide. There weren't any others. I'm not hurt." A small white lie wouldn't hurt, and something inside Serene told her to keep Dean a secret. She was still working furiously to work out his cryptic message.

Don't trust anyone? He had referred to 'these vampires'. Did that mean Stephen, Marcus, and Luke, or Hayden, Blaise, and Damian? She was sure he meant Stephen and company. She wasn't quite sure why he would prompt her not to trust them—it seemed rather apparent that they weren't to be trusted after trying to kill her twice now. But, if he meant Hayden, Blaise, and Damian, then what was he inferring?

It didn't matter. She was safe, and owed her life to Blaise and his friends. If it weren't for them, she'd have been dead by now.

"What happened to Stephen and the others?"

A shocked expression flashed on Blaise's face and it was then that it occurred to Serene that he didn't know of her encounter with them in the alley.

"How did you—"

"Last night, when I ran, I met them in an alley. They tried to kill me."

Something happened then that Serene couldn't understand. A million different thoughts seemed to mingle in Blaise's eyes, each trying to take the dominant spot, but failing. A feeling of confusion washed over her as if she was suddenly missing a crucial piece to a puzzle.

"They're dead now. I'm going to help the others clean up. Stay here."

Leaning down, his face hovered just in front of hers for a tantalizing moment before his chilled lips pressed against hers, his hand snaking around the back of her head, holding her roughly, pressing his lips harder against hers.

When their lips separated, Blaise was gone and Serene found herself collapsing onto the bed, unable to form a proper thought or recall what she had been thinking. Rolling to her side, her eyes hazed over and she worked on steadying her breathing. What had she been thinking? Her thoughts all meshed together, leaving her confused. Blaise's kiss seemed to have an hypnotic effect over her.

Minutes flew past, or so it seemed, and Blaise hadn't returned. Pushing herself from the bed, she tumbled off the side and onto her knees, placing the palm of her hand to her forehead. Shaking her head side to side, she tried to remember what was going on. Her train of thought had suddenly derailed. Flashes of memory clouded her mind. She wasn't supposed to be trusting someone. But who?

A shimmering object just below the window caught her eye. Hand. Knee. Hand. Knee. She crawled her way to the focus of her interest. Lying flat on the wooden floor was what looked like a face down picture on glossy paper, something scrawled on the back of it. Sliding her nails under the edge of the picture, she flipped it over.

A wave of memory flooded her brain. Staring up at Serene from the picture was—herself. The picture was of Serene from the other night when she returned to the house after being recaptured by Damian. Someone had been watching her? Quickly, her mind began to filter everything.

Dean. The picture must have fallen from Dean's pocket as he escaped out the window. Why did he have a picture of her though? It was like a piece to a puzzle; it didn't mean much without a million other pieces. Flipping the image over, an address was scrawled across the back in what was clearly a male's hand writing. Along with the address was Serene's name. And not just her first name; her full name. Serene Aurora Valance.

Someone was watching her, and they knew more about her than any of the others.

CHAPTER 11

After carefully hiding the tattered picture in her bag, buried deeply within her underwear, of which she hoped no one would sift through, she went in search of the others. The gory mess downstairs had been partially cleaned up by the time she arrived in the living room. A few deep red blood splatters marred the floor, but Damian was fervently scrubbing them away, his lips turned up in a snarl of disgust. Not from the sight of blood—although, that would be highly ironic—but rather from the fact that vampires were now invading his home in attempt at getting to Serene. This seemed to infuriate him to a different degree than the others, but he hid it well beneath his veiled eyes.

Days flew by and turned into weeks, with little excitement to keep Serene's mind from dwelling on the mysterious picture. Soon enough, however, she pushed it from her thoughts. Every night, she and Blaise kept to their respected sides of the bed, their bodies never touching, unless by accident; the graze of his fingers against her side or the haphazard brush of her leg against his as she battled demons in her dreams.

After being there for what seemed like ages, but was, in reality, a month, Serene was finally feeling at home. Almost. The attack had left her shaken, but Blaise had sworn to protect her and she believed him, trusted him. Life had some order to it; not that any of it made much sense. She was living with a gathering of vampires in England. If someone had told her that this is where she would have wound up, she would have laughed at them and proclaimed them mentally disturbed.

Of course, after a week, she had to write to her mother. She couldn't just disappear. Eventually, someone would recognize her and follow her, in turn, leading them to Blaise and the others. That would be a problem. Serene had written to her mother, had told her she was safe and that she would come home at the end of the summer. Whether or not she meant it was irrelevant; at least her mother would be at ease. Her cell phone was long gone, although she wasn't sure where it had gotten off to. Her only assumption was that someone had taken it and disposed of it, preventing her from making calls and exposing them. All in all, things had finally begun to calm down.

"Hi," she muttered, casting a sideways glance at him as they passed in the hallway. He ignored her and pushed into his room, disappearing from view.

Damian hadn't spoken to Serene since the attack and she couldn't decipher why. What had she done to be so ostracized by him? He exiled himself to his room much of the time now, leaving her with her muttered hellos, never even glancing up from behind his hair to acknowledge her existence. Gradually, his empty expression became tainted by pain, and each run-in they had seemed to further this agony. She couldn't tell if he was mad at her, or at himself. Either way, it caused Serene to furrow her brow in irritation.

Sighing, frustrated, she continued down the hallway, descending the staircase and skipping the last step to jump into living room, landing with a small thump on the hardwood floors, smirking as Hayden and Blaise glanced up from their hushed conversation. Everything was hushed with them these days.

Irritation must have lingered in her features.

"Still not talking to you?" Blaise inquired casually, as he did quite often lately.

"What do you think?" She knew he knew her answer. It was the same answer she had given him every day for the past three weeks. A definite, irrevocable 'No'.

"Give him time. He'll get over it."

"Get over what though?"

Her question, though she had asked it time and time again, always went unanswered as if no one ever heard her ask it.

"Just give him time." Blaise repeated, smiling at her reassuringly and patting the vacant area next to him on the couch, indicating for her to join them.

No longer hesitant like she use to be, she strode across the room and sat gracefully beside Blaise, her eyes lingering between him and Hayden. They were sharing quick glances that left Serene puzzled, but not so much as to inquire their meanings.

"How about a field trip?" Blaise looked down to Serene, a sly grin turning up the corners of his lips.

It felt like she hadn't been out of the house in ages. Not even for food. After her attempted escape, Damian had

refused to take her out again and Blaise had been too preoccupied with something he and Hayden had been working on.
Whenever someone went out they brought back food and that
seemed to suffice.

"I need to go to the book store," chimed Blaise, rising from
his seat and pivoting to Serene, waiting.

The book store.

The last time she had seen the dust laden windows of the
store was the night she had nearly escaped this nightmare,
although her 'nightmare' was slowly transforming into a
dream. Nothing seemed to have changed. The window display
was still the same arrangement of books with the same sheet
of dust clouding their surfaces. Spider webs, although much
larger now, still clung to the pane of glass and surrounding
wood, small flies wrapped tightly in the fine fibers. It was still
dark, if not darker, and there was no evidence of anyone
entering or exiting. How unnerving.

The inside wasn't any different either. What was with this
place? Most of the book stores that Serene knew of back home
were constantly rearranging everything, making way for the
newest books. The contents of this store looked like they
hadn't been changed in decades; like the books had been sitting on the shelves since they were written. How could a place
this barren survive as a business?

Not a single customer occupied the store, as opposed to last
time when she had taken the liberty of watching Barbie and
Goth Chick roam up and down the isles. However, much like
last time, a shadow shifted from the back of the longest isle,
keeping tight to the bookshelf and just out of view of Serene.

Blaise stepped forward, his fingers brushing against her arm as he did so. His eyes swivelled to her.

"Don't leave."

"I won't," she answered with earnest eyes.

With a blurred motion, his lips were just next to her ear, hot breath blowing down her neck. "Promise me."

Her breath caught in her throat and she swallowed, dizzied by his actions.

"I promise."

He was gone before she could even finish, disappearing toward the shadow and slinking into the back room, just as Damian had done the first time they were here.

The back room was a mystery. What was back there that seemed to lure in the vampires? And who or what was the mysterious shadow constantly lurking about the book store, always present but never seen? Thinking back on it, Serene realized that Hayden and Blaise's hushed conversations had begun after she and Damian had returned from the book store. Was there some secretive vampire meeting behind the closed doors?

Blaise appeared, emerging from the obscure black hole behind the rugged door, the shadow sulking out behind him. Blaise's eyes locked with hers from the end of the isle, warning her with a sharp gaze to stay put. Responding with a curt nod, her sharp green eyes watched him carefully as he and the figure passed each isle, disappearing through another door.

Instantly, her eyes snapped to the run-down door. Without consciously realizing it, her feet began to shuffle, carrying her further and further from her promised location and closer and closer to the back room. Closing the distance between herself and the door, she noted that the doorknob was rusted

in several places. A small keyhole signified that the knob must
have been centuries old. She hadn't seen styles like it anywhere with the exception of old-fashion movies. It was the
kind of keyhole that little kids would peek through to spy on
unsuspecting victims in the opposing room.

The door stood ajar. How convenient. How alluring. How
damn tempting it was for Serene to just slip inside, just for a
moment, to quench her curiosity. Nothing was visible
through the slit in the door. Just an obscure blackness, seemingly endless. With a second of hesitation and a quick glance
over her shoulder, she slid into the room, closing the door
soundlessly behind her.

Dark. Very dark. Reaching out in front of her, her hands
swished through the air, grasping for something to hold onto
while making sure she didn't run head on into a wall. One
step. Two steps. Three steps. Four steps.

Five steps. Small, black candles sparked to life all around
the room, casting the smallest of shadows and illuminating
everything with a golden glow.

Furrowing her brow, Serene looked around at the occult-
like decor. Candles were seemingly the only source of light;
there were no lamps or light switches to be found. A circular,
black rug covered most of the floor, save for the corners which
were furry with dust. A long, mahogany table was pressed
against the north wall, books and papers piled in stacks. At
the center of the table sat a thick, leather-bound book that,
unlike the massive piles surrounding it, sat perched on a
stand, slightly elevated from the chaos. The walls were made
of dingy brick, chips and holes peppering the red stone.

Advancing to the table, Serene ran her hand along the dark
wood, almost awed by the gothic beauty of the room. Papers

were sprawled out in an unorganized frenzy. Scanning the slips, she noted that most, if not all of them, were names. An occasional address was tossed in here and there, but for the most part it was names. Some were mere crumbled post-its. Other's were lists, made up of two or three pages of names upon names.

None of this struck Serene as important. Perhaps it was a list of frequent buyers? Although she wasn't sure this store even knew of the term 'frequent buyer'. Her eyes diverted from the lists and fell on the leather book. It had no inscriptions on it nor any locks. It looked like it could be a large journal of some sort, but she wasn't entirely sure. Running her finger tips along the edge of the leather, she opened it.

Photos. It was a photo album. All of the pictures were similar. Each of them was a candid shot. There was nothing distinguishing about the people. They were each doing something insignificant. Something totally normal as if they weren't aware that they were being photographed.

Something inside of Serene's head snapped together.

"There is a supplier at the book store that keeps a list of known criminals in the area."

Blaise had told her that the first night she spent with him. Now that she thought about it, he had explained this all to her before. She recalled vaguely that the dealer worked back here, supplying them with the names they needed. Looking down at the pictures, it donned on her that each of these people were criminals; food for the vampires. The lists must be the names and addresses of mortals that they could hunt freely, without hesitation or remorse.

Flipping through the pages, it sickened her to know that all of these people would be murdered someday, sucked dry because of their crimes. Men and woman. Adults and teens. Black and white. There was nothing defining about these people; nothing sinister in their looks that would label them as criminals, yet there they were, unknowingly being hunted because of their sins.

Nobility took over Serene. She felt that if she saved one of their lives, she would be doing all that she could. Even if they were criminals, she found it wrong to offer them up as vampire bait. She'd take one picture, just one, and save that poor soul from an untimely demise.

Flipping lazily through the pages, she tried to pick the person that looked the least threatening. The problem was, none of these people looked remotely dangerous to her. There was a slender, Asian woman, tending to her garden. There was a brawny young man, no older than thirty, reading a newspaper at a local park. But what had these people done? There was nothing to inform her of their crimes. No labels or side notes. Nothing. She'd have to follow her gut instinct.

The loud thumping of footsteps sounded from just outside the door and began moving off down the isle. Her heart leapt to her throat. If Blaise thought she'd left—she didn't even want to think about the outcome. Quickly, and without looking, she grabbed a picture from the photo album, closed it, and hurried across the room, shoving the picture deep within her pocket. Slipping out, she left the door ajar, just as she had found it, and carefully slunk down an isle of books.

Hurried footsteps shook the floor beneath her and she rounded to face a shelf of books, a plan quickly springing to her mind.

Blaise appeared just beside her, glowering down at her with clenched teeth.

"Doesn't this book look great?" Serene questioned, smiling as she plucked a thick black book from the dusty shelves and holding it up to Blaise. *Five Hundred Ways to Vanquish A Demon.* Oh god. He'd never believe that she was actually interested in this book.

Fury quickly faded from his eyes, replaced with amusement as he grasped the book.

"I know you told me to wait there, but you took so long and I got bored. Decided to do some quick browsing."

Lies. Bold-faced lies, but he'd never know.

"Hmm. You like this book?" He looked at her skeptically, but as she nodded he smiled. "Well, then. That's settled."

Striding down the isle, away from Serene, he smirked. Following quickly, Serene practically had to jog to match his speed. When she emerged from the isle, her eyes fell on Blaise, grasping a plastic bag being handed to him by the cashier. With a muttered thank you, he turned to Serene with a smile.

"Here you are." He handed her the bag. "We should be heading back now. Don't want Damian to think you ran off again."

Hayden was still entirely unaware of her attempted dash to freedom. She wasn't sure why the others hadn't told him, but she assumed it was for her own safety. While Hayden may be kind, he had obligations as the leader to protect himself and his family. And, with Alaria still in Russia, he didn't want to give her any reason to come back and off Serene.

Clutching the bag, she peered inside. *Five Hundred Ways to Vanquish A Demon* clung to the plastic bag, a receipt visible just beside it.

The picture was of a young, blonde girl, no older than eighteen. Decked in a skirt and white t-shirt, she was walking down the street, her hand laced with that of a boy's. Young love. What could this angel faced girl have done that was so dreadful as to land her on the list in the back of the book store?

Sitting at the edge of Blaise's bed, she starred down at the two pictures; herself and the blonde. The way the pictures looked, the style in which they were done, the candidness of the shots; they looked as if they were taken by the same person. Serene, puzzled, eyed the pictures side by side. She couldn't be sure, but the two pictures definitely looked like they were caught by the same person. The angles were the same, the distances were similar, even the quality of the two prints were identical.

"Serene?"

Hearing her name being called, Serene quickly scrambled to the closet and shoved the pictures into her bag before quietly closing the door. Just as she spun around, Blaise entered, eyeing her with a puzzled expression before a smirk slid across his face.

"I'm going to bed. Care to join?"

CHAPTER 12

Getting ready for bed was a well-known routine now. Blaise turned his back to Serene and she quickly disrobed before scurrying into her pajamas, always attentive to Blaise, making sure he didn't steal a glimpse without her knowledge. When she was done, she'd pace to her side of the bed, her footsteps a signal for Blaise to turn.

Pulling back the covers, Blaise always laid down first, an angelic blur as he shifted beneath the sheets, folding them down to expose his sculpted chest and rock hard abs; his physique intensified by the pale shading of his skin. Serene would follow suit, being careful not to make contact with him as she clambered into bed, pulling the covers well up to her chin.

Tonight was different however. Standing on his side of the bed, Blaise shot a glance at Serene, his eyes than trailing to the bed as if insisting that she crawl in first. Watching him with an inquisitive expression, she pulled back the covers, her hand knotting tightly around the thick fabric.

Gliding between the sheet and the comforter, her skin was overly sensitive to the Egyptian Cotton that molded to her form. Blaise pulled his shirt over his head, his motions flowing as he slipped off his shoes and socks. Swiftly, he slid out of his jeans, revealing a pair of black boxers that sent butterflies flying through Serene's stomach. She watched Blaise as he slid in next to her, his spellbinding blue eyes locking into her green gaze with such intensity that looking away was impossible.

Slowly, unknowingly, Serene slid toward him and his arms snaked around her body, pulling her closer. His skin was like ice against hers, but blood rushed furiously through her body sending heat waves across the two of them. Heart racing, she stared into his eyes, her fingers hesitantly rising to his face and tracing down his jaw line. He was amazing. It was amazing the way his body, so strong and built, seemed to curve perfectly against hers, so weak and petite.

His lips grazed the hollow of her neck, sending chills down her spine. Her hand ran up the side of his face, her fingers gently tracing the contours of his features. Breathing seemed to be a foreign concept; Serene couldn't tell if she was taking in oxygen or not. Smirking, Blaise leaned in and set his chilled pale lips roughly against hers. Indulged in the moment, she looped her arms around his neck and held herself closer to him. Blaise pulled back and set his lips beside her ear, a hot puff of breath crawling down her neck.

"I love you, Serene."

The instance the words left his mouth, Serene felt repelled. She pulled back, her arms snapping to her sides and her eyes growing distant. It was apparent by the perplexed look on Blaise's face that he had not been expecting her reaction. Eyeing her, he reached out, but she shifted away again, tossing on a smile for his sake.

"Goodnight, Blaise." She set a soft kiss on his cheek, moved toward him once again, and turned her back to him.

Cocking an eyebrow, anger radiated from Blaise. Her reaction was all wrong. Whatever had just happened was beyond him.

Blaise wrapped one arm around Serene's waist to hold her close, breathing in the scent of her hair as he drifted to sleep beside her.

Sheets snaked around her legs, constricting her to the bed and leaving red marks on her skin. Waking up was difficult. Serene hadn't slept so well in a long time. Blaise's arm was secured around her waist, even as she began to stir. Despite the heap of blankets encasing them, his body was frigid against her flushed skin. Once again, things were different. Blaise's body beside hers as she awoke was unusual. Turning in his arms, her eyes met his, awake and staring with a sly grin, teasing her.

"Morning," he breathed, tucking a strand of her auburn hair behind her ear.

"Hi." Smiling sheepishly, she parted herself from him and untangled her legs, readjusting herself, perching on her side of the bed.

"Sleep well?"

"Mhmm." Biting her lip, she moved from the bed, constantly aware of his eyes piercing the air and following her every movement.

Sitting up, Blaise brought his hand through his hair, muscles stretching down his torso as he stirred.

"Excuse me while I change. By the way, you look beautiful when you sleep."

He was gone, his words trailing behind him like a ghostly echo.

Having a moment alone, Serene's mind began to wander, lingering on the previous night. Love. *I love you, Serene.* How could he love her? How? They had only known each other for a month or so, yet already Serene felt as comfortable with him as she had with Ben, perhaps even more-so. Cradling her head in her hands, sounds and images danced within her head. Could she love Blaise? Could she love him and the monster that he was? Her mother had warned her about boys, but not of the hunky vampire variety.

For a girl of seventeen, she was facing issues that were well beyond her years. Love. Boys. Vampires. And on top of everything, she was faced with the fact that someone was watching her; knew all about her.

Someone out there was paying very close attention to her and the company she kept, but why? Nothing made sense to her. There were bits and pieces of a puzzle, all stretched out in front of her, but something was missing. A key piece to the mystery wasn't there, and she had no way of finding it.

Rising from the bed, Serene went to the closet and pulled out her bag. Digging through the clothing, she located the two photographs and returned to the bed, her eyes flashing between the two pictures, trying to make some sense of it all.

Both were similar, both were candid shots, and both were printed on—glossy paper.

A spark ignited in her mind. Glossy paper. She titled the pictures this way and that in the gleam of the bedside lamp, watching the paper reflect a glare that sparkled in her eyes.

Her mind took her back to that day in Hayden's room. She had seen a glimmer just like that shining from within his beside table. It could all just be a coincidence, but it suddenly became very clear to Serene that she needed to ascertain whatever it was that resided in Hayden's bedside table.

Her normal morning routine was rushed as she slid in and out of the shower, pulled on a change of clothes and left the bathroom slightly unorganized. After checking the hall for any signs of Hayden or Blaise, she snuck down the hall toward Hayden's room. Reaching Blaise's room, she paused just outside the door to listen for his presence. After a moment or two of silence, she passed and finished off the length of the hallway.

The door, unlike last time, was closed. Glancing over her shoulder, she wondered if Hayden was in his room. It would be a death threat to just walk in. Turning her eyes back to the wooden door, she raised her hand, curled it into a fist, and reluctantly knocked. Her stomach knotted up as anxiety bubbled up within her. A moment passed and no one answered, sending a wave of relief over Serene.

Gnawing on the inside of her lip, she grasped the rustic doorknob and jiggled it. Unlocked. Sighing, she pushed the door open and slid inside quickly, closing the door behind her with a hushed click as she turned the lock. Better safe than sorry. Moving with slow, steady motions, she approached the bedside table, her eyes and ears alert to any movement or sound. The slightest creak of a floorboard was enough to send Serene's eyes into a frantic race to locate the culprit.

The room hadn't changed, making her plan simple and accurate. Without further hesitation, she strode to the bedside table, her eyes zoning in on the drawer which was now closed and, to her dismay, locked. The drawer consisted of a keyhole much like the one in the door.

"Damn." Cursing under her breath, she sneered at the cause of her frustration. Why would Hayden lock the drawer? Probably because he caught Serene in his room the last time, headed toward the same drawer. So what was he hiding? The obvious effort to keep her out drove Serene to anger, a sudden passion for discovering the truth boiling up within her.

Where would Hayden be hiding the key? A good question, but Serene couldn't seem to place the answer. Time was always against her these days. Quickly, she began a search, moving in a square pattern around the room. It wasn't under the bed or the table. It wasn't inside of the dresser, closet, or wooden jewelry box. It wasn't even stashed under the frame of the bed. Standing with her back against the bedroom door, her green eyes pierced the room, contemplating her remaining choices. Slowly, as if a force had directed her eyes, she zoned in on a portrait of Hayden and Alaria, hung high about the bed's headboard.

It would be rather late 1800's of Hayden to hide the key behind the back of the portrait. It was one of those hiding places that you'd only think about in a cheesy mystery novel. But choices were limited and Serene was running out of time. Inching toward the bed, she used the side of it as a support for her knees. With an elongated grasp, she slid her hand behind the portrait, nerves eating away at her as the painted eyes of Hayden and Alaria followed her. And, just as she had thought, the tips of her fingers stroked something cold; something metal. Digging it up with her nails, she pulled out a small, sliver key.

Her lips turned up into an excited grin as she clambered off the bed and sunk to her knees before the table. Sliding the key into the keyhole, her heart raced as it fit and she began to slowly turn it. With a barely audible click, the drawer came loose and Serene pulled it open, standing to scan its contents.

Pictures. Dozens and dozens of pictures sprawled out in all directions within the drawer, each glimmering in the light of the lamp, producing the same shimmer as the others.

Digging through the photos, Serene pulled out pile after pile and set them on the bed, spreading them out to examine them. A sickening sensation came over her as she stared in horror at the snapshots. Just like the others, they were candid; taken of random people at random moments.

Her eyes began to well up with tears as she looked on. Priests, children, mothers and fathers, grandmothers and grandfathers. Couples on the way to the store, a pair decked out for their wedding, teens laughing with one another on their way to a football game. These people didn't resemble criminals. They didn't look dangerous and cynical. These people weren't criminals at all. They were innocent.

Hayden. Blaise. Damian. Alaria. They weren't killing those who deserved it. They were killing everyone, good and bad. Everything about the dealer that supplied them with criminals; it was all a lie. They weren't good vampires. They weren't doing justice to the name of vampires. They were cold-blooded killers and she was stuck in their game.

Hastily pulling the two previous pictures from her pocket, she flipped them over. Her mind clicked through images, placing things together in a frantic moment of understanding. Turning over numerous other pictures, her stomach flipped.

Writing. There was writing on the back of each of them. Names, addresses. Everything was written by the same hand—even her own name scrawled across the back of her picture. Someone wanted her dead, just like the victims in these photos. Dean had been in possession of her photo, linking him to the conspiracy. She didn't know who was after her or why they wanted her dead, but she did know one thing.

Hayden and the others were all in on it.

CHAPTER 13

Terror stricken by her recent discoveries, Serene's mind began to spin, formulating what she hoped would be a flawless plan, although she wasn't counting on it. One thing was certain; she needed to get as far away from the house as possible. Where she would go was not of concern at the moment. The only thing on her mind was getting out and away without being detected.

I could climb out the bedroom window. Dean did it. So could I.

It seemed like a perfect escape route. Out the bedroom window, down the siding of the house, and safely across the lawn where she would disappear into the surrounding neighborhood and seek safety.

Her error proof plan came to a grinding halt as two icy arms snaked around her, one latching around her waist, the other smothering her mouth. Being pulled tightly against the figure, she struggled; a fruitless effort. With sharp motions, a pair of lips parted beside her ear.

"Don't struggle. Don't scream. There isn't enough time. Hayden already knows you've found out. He'll be here in seconds. Just trust me, Serene."

His voice, though she hadn't heard it in a little over a month, was familiar; alarming and soothing simultaneously. Tentatively, he slid his hand from her mouth, relocating to a firm grip on her shoulder. It reminded her of the first time they had met, when he had been forcing her down the darkened hallway to her holding chamber.

Spinning to face Damian, her eyes searched for his but found his black curtain of hair masking his emotions. Once, just once, she'd like to be able to stare into his exotic, violet eyes and make sense of what she found there.

With unnatural speed, they glided to the window.

"Now I know why the doors seem so unused," she mused in a hushed tone. Wrong time for jokes judging by the bewildered glare sent her way.

The window opened willingly, nearly being yanked from its frame in Damian's hurry. The ledge just outside the window was an inch or two thick; hardly big enough to perch on. Serene stuck her head warily out the window, taking in the distance from them to the ground. Not life threatening heights, but bone shattering none-the-less. Inching away from the open window, she shook her head.

A disoriented sensation filled her body as she was suddenly pushed out the window, Damian's arms forming a protective steel cage around her as he rolled, turning his back to the ground. A moment later and a booming thud ricocheted through Serene's ears. With blurred speed, Damian had her on her feet. A human impacting the ground with such force would have shattered many bones in their body, but Damian seemed virtually unscathed. The only evidence of the fall was his imprint in the soggy grass.

Wide-eyed with fear and confusion, Serene was jostled as Damian yanked her away from the scene, moving stealthily toward the street. Where could they possibly go that would be secure? Was there anywhere in the world that Hayden and Blaise couldn't find her? Distrust for Damian edged her mind, but she didn't have time to think it over. It was either test her fate with him or try and escape on her own. Damian seemed more promising.

He must have decided early on that taking his car was problematic; trackers were probably laced through the automobiles parts, in the off chance that Damian went missing and needed to be found. As a substitute, he promptly chose to hijack a sleek, black XKR Jaguar Coupe. Serene didn't know much about cars, but from what she *did* know the car was fast, reliable, and expensive. She almost felt bad for the owner of the breathtaking vehicle. It was almost certain that they would not be seeing their car again. Pity.

Luck was on their side; the car doors were unlocked. Serene's world spun sideways, being tossed into the passenger seat, Damian appearing next to her a moment later, his fingers already fast at work on the car's ignition. A blue tool clutched in his hand, he set it in the ignition and jerked at the bar of metal. Catching Serene's inquisitive gaze, he narrowed his eyes on the task at hand.

"Slide-hammer. Found it in the trunk. Normally it's used for dents, but it happens to be handy for hot-wiring cars." The ignition came ripping out, a sprawl of wires following. Two red wires seemed to catch his interest and he set to work on crossing them. Within seconds the car purred to life.

Night had fallen upon them like a blanket, softening the edges of the surrounding world and building walls of endless darkness in the corners of Serene's all too human vision. They had been driving for what seemed like hours. The digital clock, showering green light from its digits, claimed it to be nine thirty-five, PM. They had been on the road for quite some time, silence clinging to the atmosphere, leaving Serene with her thoughts.

Blaise had claimed to love her, but his words had been lies; a faux portrayal of emotions. He had created a tantalizing illusion that had, until now, captivated her. This was precisely why Serene was guarded when it came to love. Trust and love did not sit well with her, and the situation at hand only furthered her wariness. Why trust an emotion that could mar your heart for life? Her fear of letting someone in ultimately pushed them away. It had happened with Ben. And now, when her guards were slowly receding, a harsh lie shattered her naive mind set, her shields being thrown back up.

Now nothing made sense. Damian hadn't spoken to her since the attack, yet unexpectedly he was rescuing her? None of it added up and it was eating away at Serene. How could she possible trust Damian with such lack of insight to the situation? Questions boggled her mind, but it seemed the wrong time to ask them.

Daring to steal a sideways glance at Damian, she noted his expression; pained. The same expression he had carried when they would spot each other in passing. Anger mingled with confusion in her subconscious mind. What could she have possibly done to strike suck agony to his chiseled features? She held her eyes on him, but he maintained an intent focus on the black tar ahead of them. Driving without headlights on,

Serene saw nothing, but Damian's eyes could see just as clearly as if it were midday.

The car was fast, but evidently not fast enough for Damian who seemed positively irritated as he pushed the gauge to its limits and found himself unsatisfied. It was apparent that he was worried. Worried about betraying his friends; his clan. Worried about escaping, about putting enough distance between Serene and the others in the little time he had. Damian took the saying "put the pedal to the metal" quite literally, the steel gas pedal clinking against the floor of the car. It was unnerving for Serene, not being able to see the road, but knowing that Damian was speeding far above the limit in his rush to get her to safety.

Jolting upright, Serene gasped. Her skin crawled as a maddening silence filled her ears and heat washed over her like a blanket, thick and warm—much too warm for the interior of the car. The cushioned mattress below her, molding to her curves, didn't exactly scream car either.

Shifting, a timber wall met her gaze. After coming to the blatant conclusion that she was no longer in the car, she sat up, peering through the darkness, wishing she had night vision. After a moment or so, her eyes adjusted to the obscurity and specks of moonlight breaking through the blackened windows provided just enough light to make out her surroundings.

The walls were that of a decayed cabin with rustic decor and dust laden windows. The beaten floor was shrouded with a mud-laced rug. Firewood was piled in the corner, waiting eagerly to be charred by the brick fireplace a mere foot away. With the edge of the quilt she found clinging to her body

Serene wiped a circle of dust from the window. Tree branches rested against the thin pane of glass, bending in protest to the window preventing their expansion.

Where am I? What the hell is going on?

Thoughts bounced around the interior of Serene's mind. Last she recalled she had been in the car, steadily growing drowsy. Sleep must have taken her, but that didn't explain where she was. Another good question, where was Damian? Surely he hadn't left her here alone? Unless Damian wasn't the one who had taken her here. Maybe, in her sleeping state, the car had been ambushed and she was currently unknowingly prisoner to whoever it was that was after her.

These thoughts were resolved as Damian's toned figure came striding through the door, a steaming plate clutched in his hands. Without a glance to Serene, he set the plate of food down on a small, rigid table beside the bed.

"Eat," he grunted, his tone rough and edgy, filled with complication.

A pile of french-fries sent small wisps of steam into the air, mixing with the already stifling heat of the cabin. A black unit heater, positioned strategically beside the bed, was the culprit of the heat. Suddenly, without warning, a furious wave of heat wavered through the room. Cocking her head, she spotted Damian feeding a now blazing fire with logs. Fixing him with a vexed stared, Serene, agitated, kicked off the quilt that was threatening to suffocate her in her overheated state.

"Eat." No longer a grunt, his tone was almost pleading.

Taking a liking to the floor, Damian sat at the edge of the rug, gazing into the fire as the flames danced and licked up the corners of the wood, the light illuminating his body faintly, casting a shadow across the room.

Sighing in frustration, Serene obeyed his plead and picked at a french-fry, taking her time nibbling at the steaming food. Watching Damian was like observing a rare species of animal. His expressions shifted so quickly that it was hard to depict the movie of feelings flashing across his face. Anger. Sadness. Regret. What was it that caused this display of perturbation?

Discreetly, after finishing off another fry, Serene clambered off the bed, traipsed across the rug and sat down gingerly beside Damian, locking her eyes on the fire in fear of catching a stern glare from him.

Feeling her presence next to him, anger boiled beneath Damian's skin and a wave a fury suddenly filled his thoughts.

"You should never have come to the house with Blaise. What were you thinking? You're so naive!" he hissed, his eyes narrowing to slits, glaring at the fire

Taken aback, Serene turned her head to him so fast that it nearly gave her whiplash.

"Why do you hate me?" she demanded, fury cutting her words like a knife.

"I don't hate you!" he roared, rounding on her, his violet eyes blazing from behind his black hair with such rage that Serene scooted back a bit. With a lunge, Damian grabbed her by she shoulders and, with a streak of motion, had her on her feet and pushed against the wall. "Don't you get it? I don't hate you! I care too much about you to hate you! I—" his words broke off and Serene stared at him, fear stricken, her body trembling against the wall.

"I'm sorry. I'm-sorry." Damian released her and she sunk to the floor, her back dragging down the wall. Stepping back, he held his eyes on her, appalled at his actions. With a good ten feet between them, he sunk to the floor as well, his eyes bewildered at his reaction, his face pain stricken. Emotional pain.

"I'm sorry," he repeated, his tone defeated.

The world had titled on its axis, confusing everything Serene had thought she had figured out. If Damian didn't hate her than why was he so bitter toward her? Why had he spent so much time ignoring her if he cared about her well-being? And most importantly, why had he been helping Blaise and Hayden trick her if he didn't want her harmed? With puzzled green eyes, she inched away from the corner, crawling to his disheartened figure sitting on the floor a few feet away.

"Damian, I—" she trailed off. What did she want to say? What could she possibly say to make sense of this?

"This wasn't supposed to happen this way. I wasn't supposed to—you weren't supposed to—" his words made little sense, his sentences broken and incoherent.

Just an inch from him, Serene timidly reached out and set her hand on top of his, cold against the floor. "What's happening Damian? Why did you bring me here?"

Locking his eyes with hers, he shook his head slowly, not knowing what to tell her. None of this was supposed to have happened. He wasn't supposed to be feeling the way he was feeling toward her and she wasn't supposed to trust him like she did. It had all been planned out, but not a single thing had worked out the way it was meant to.

"We were hired. Hired to kidnap you and keep you alive. Don't you get it, Serene? Everything has been planned. Fixed. Meeting Blaise on the plane. Falling in what you thought was love with him; vampire magic. The attack on the house by Stephen, Marcus and Luke. Dean. None of it was real."

"It was all a set up; a ploy."

CHAPTER 14

Her stomach knotted repeatedly as he spoke, a sickened, horrified sensation drowning her. How could this be happening? She had figured out that something wasn't right the moment she discovered the pictures of the innocent victims. But everything? A trick? Why?

"We knew you were coming to England. Blaise had been watching you in Covington for a week. He was sent to meet you on the plane. He was supposed to make you trust him, help you transition into England safely. When he got you to the house he had second thoughts, but he was too weak minded to turn back. You followed him in, just as we knew you would. That's when things began to go wrong. Alaria was appalled, more so than we thought she might be, and she left. She wanted to kill you then and there, but that was against order. It wasn't a problem, so we kept up the charade." Damian watched her with careful eyes, regret and remorse lacing his words.

"When you ran from me at the book store I tried not to find you. I was ready to let you go, to let you live, but I sensed you in the alley with Stephen, Marcus, and Luke. I knew they were working for us, but I knew they'd kill you on the spot despite our commands. I had no choice but to save you and bring you back. It didn't take long for you to fall for Blaise. I had my doubts. I thought you were stronger than that, but his magic was too intense for you. Once he had your trust he knew you wouldn't try to run again. Then all we had to do was set a false sense of security. That's why we hired Stephen and his crew to attack. We needed you to trust us, to think that we'd protect you at all costs." He paused, prying his gaze from her and staring intensely at the fire, pulling his hand from beneath hers and setting it to his side.

"That's when I started realizing how frightened the thought of you in danger made me. I knew that the only way I'd be able to go through with this was if I distanced myself from you. That's why I stopped talking to you. Not because I hated you, because I cared too much for you. Because I—" He stopped and his expression portrayed such agony that it made Serene's eyes water.

"Another mistake was made, but this time it caused a problem, one that none of us had seen coming. Dean. He works in the back of the book store. He's the one who provides us with humans to feed from; he's the shadow you saw in the back isle. As you've noticed, some humans work for us. Well, that day at the attack he made a fatal mistake by warning you and dropping your picture on his way out the window. You see, Dean doesn't just work for us. He works for our employer as well and he's been watching you. That's how he got your picture; just like he got the rest of the pictures. Blaise had sensed him in the room when he came to check on you."

"Everyone knew that Dean had to be taken care of. He was too human; too caring. And then Blaise took you to the book store again. He killed Dean that day, under strict orders from

Hayden. We couldn't risk any more mistakes. Blaise said that you'd been acting peculiar when he found you looking at some books, but it didn't connect until much later that day. When he realized that you had been in the back room he was mystified. How could a mortal girl, so weak and simple minded, break through his magic and disobey his orders? Plans were put into action to take you to our employer. I overheard Blaise and Hayden whispering in the living room. By that time, you had already discovered Hayden's pictures. Before Hayden had a chance to react I knew I had to get you out of there. It was a split second reaction, but I made up my mind. I had to save you."

Serene sat in silence, terrified by his tale. They had known her before she had known them. Someone had set this all up; she had been unknowingly kidnaped the moment she met Blaise on the plane. They had lured her to their home and made her feel comfortable, safe. Blaise had even made her feel for him things she had only ever felt for Ben and then some.

However, their plan was set off course when Dean warned her, his human emotions getting the better of him and ultimately killing him. And then the pictures—all of the pictures. After putting two and two together Serene had figured that she was living with murderers. It bewildered her to hear that such an intricate plan had been set up merely for the purpose of containing her. But what was the purpose of holding her captive? Why not just kill her? What were they waiting for?

"Why? Why not just k-kill me?" Goose bumps rose up her body at her own voice, broken and horrified.

Damian turned from the fire and peered out from behind his veil of hair, apologizing eyes melting into her.

"I can't answer that because I don't know. Being the youngest, I wasn't told everything. All I know is that we were instructed to find you and keep you until told otherwise. Whoever is behind all of this knew where we could find you. Whoever it is knew you were coming to England."

Stopping, he reached out, grasping her hand. "It's dangerous for you now. Whoever it is that gave us our orders, they aren't going to be happy now that you have escaped. The vampire behind this must be very powerful if they're controlling Hayden. You are no longer safe, Serene."

Everything was slowly melting together in her mind, image after image, fact after fact. Blaise and Hayden were the culprits here and Damian was simply too young to rebel against them—but he did. He revolted against their plans and helped Serene escape.

Poor Dean had died in his efforts to rescue her, to warn her. And all of this, the elaborate planning, the lies and false sense of security, all of it was because somewhere out there was a powerful vampire, controlling them and guiding them, making them keep Serene. But why? Even Damian couldn't answer that question.

"I don't know how long we'll be safe here. We have a better chance without Alaria on their side. She's still in Russia last I heard. They'll come looking for us soon enough if they aren't already on their way, so we can stay here tonight, but tomorrow we move."

"Tonight we feast." With a laugh he stood. Serene blinked and he was gone, blurring back into view a moment later, grasping the still steaming plate of french-fries and sitting back down.

"On french-fries?"

"On french-fries," he confirmed.

That night Serene was witness to a very different Damian. He talked and laughed and, for the first time since she had met him, his eyes weren't fully hidden behind his veil of hair. It was odd seeing him so—human.

And as the night wore on Serene became intensely aware of the security she felt around him. It was much like how she had felt with Blaise, but three times greater. There was an aggressive aura about Damian. He was wild, unpredictable, and struck fear through her with just the right look, but despite her common sense, she trusted him.

Small talk and laughter carried them through the night until, just a few hours before dawn, fatigue took Serene, sending her into a deep, dreamless sleep.

Damian sat with his back to the wall opposite the bed, his violet eyes penetrating the room, boring into Serene as he examined her motionless figure. So frail. So delicate. So easily broken. To him, Serene's bones were like twigs beneath his fingers. And though he'd never hurt her, there were now two groups of vampires prowling nearby, hunting. Serene was their prey and Damian her only means of protection.

With dawn came golden beams of light just barely filtering through the grimy windows. Shifting from the shadows in the corner, Damian glared and directed his attention to the pile of blankets stirring on the bed. Out came a hand, and a foot, and finally a head.

A groggy looking Serene muttered, shielding her eyes from the unwelcome beams of light. Unwelcome on both accounts.

"Seems the weather has decided to betray us today." Damian released a low growl as he paced across the room to where she lay.

"So I've noticed," she grumbled, slinking back beneath the covers.

A smile flitted across his visage before quickly disappearing. With one swift tug the blanket flew from her form, crumpling to the floor to reveal Serene with an incredibly vexed grimace.

"You don't see *me* yanking *you* out of bed, do you?"

With no response, he stood and took a fleeting glance out the window. Sun poured through the dirt free spots.

"The rain chose today as its day off," sighed Damian, sitting on the edge of the bed, chagrin etched into his features. "We'll have to wait until the sun goes down or, with some luck, it begins to rain again."

"Why? Blaise told me that the sun doesn't kill you. That it just—"

"Irritates our skin. Yes, but I'd like to wait it out if at all possible."

Nodding in understanding, Serene hopped off the bed and stumbled over to the oak-rimmed window on the far wall. Setting her palm against the cold surface, she wiped away a circle and peered out, eager to feel the warmth of sun against her flesh.

As if the window had burned her, she gasped and backed away, stumbling over the corner of the carpet, her voice squeaking out nervously.

"I don't think we have time to wait it out, Damian," whispered Serene.

"Why's that?" he questioned, almost amused as his eyes traced the patterns in the carpet.

"Because," she paused, turning to him with horror-struck eyes. "Someone is outside the cabin."

CHAPTER 15

With a lurch, Damian sprang from the bed, blurring to the window while avoiding the rouge beams of light penetrating the decrepit glass. His eyes could see much clearer than Serene's and would also pick up any sign of body heat within one hundred yards—built-in infrared. A few small, red forms burned through the tress. Squirrels, birds, and a slew of other animals, but nothing human, which alarmed him. If Serene *had* seen someone, they were no longer living. That eliminated hunters or teens out on a hike, and left the presumed—vampires.

Movement from Serene caught Damian's eye and he held a finger to her, rooting her to the spot. His eyes grew dark and his body ran rigid. Complete silence took the room. Serene even held her breath for the moment, watching Damian attentively, trying to decipher exactly what it was he was doing.

With enough luck and patience, Damian hoped that he could pick up sound waves from the approaching threat. A sniffle, a sigh, a twig snap, anything that might give him an inkling of a clue as to who it was and which direction they were closing in from.

A sharp bang from the room to the right was a sure fire signal that they had officially run out of time.

Scrambling toward Damian, Serene stared in horror as a second thump announced the entrance of not one, but two attackers. An arm coiled around her waist, Damian's arm, and they were in motion.

Slamming through the oak door, sun rained down on them, Damian's face contorting into a sneer. His skin danced in the radiance of the beams, tingling like an immediate sunburn, unseen but irritating. Time was slipping through their fingers. They had to move. Fast.

Thunderous footsteps from within the cabin played as a catalyst, sending Damian hurtling into the woods, Serene tightly in his grasp, her feet never touching the ground. The shade of the trees was just enough to shield Damian from the unrelenting sun. Now and then a stray ray would break through the branches overhead and strike him, causing hisses of pain. Serene clung to him as they shifted through the mass of trees, twigs snagging on her hair and clothes.

They were moving fast, but not fast enough. Glancing over Damian's shoulder, Serene caught two shadows advancing through the brush. Fear crippled her. She clenched her hands, her fingers digging into Damian's biceps. Shifting her, his arms tightened around her waist, her feet riding on his. Leaves kicked up in a whirl wind of chaos beneath Damian, settling back on the ground soon after, disturbed.

"You're leaving a trail," Serene whimpered in his ear, her eyes widening at the line of leaves behind them.

"That's the plan," he stated matter-of-factly.

He wanted them to follow? Why? That didn't make much sense.

It took but a moment for things to pan out, providing somewhat of an explanation. With a lurch, they were hurtling through the air, upwards. Serene gasped and Damian's palm quickly covered her mouth, keeping her from screaming.

Tree branches flew past in Serene's peripheral vision. He had jumped much higher than any normal person could have, even with the assistance of a trampoline. With the grace of an eagle swooping in for a landing, Damian set his feet firmly on one of the most sheltered branches, perching effortlessly, Serene still in his grasp. He kept her silenced as he ran rigid once again, his ears like a sonar, scanning the surrounding areas. In a moments time he froze, his eyes narrowing and gazing down through the thick branches.

Though Serene's eyes couldn't make out what was going on through the thicket of trees below, she could hear voices. Two of them conversing in hushed whispers, but now and then a fragment of a sentence or two would break through the sound barrier of tree limbs and meet her ears.

"-just disappear like that? He doesn't have that power."

"But the trail ends—."

"-turned back I guess."

"—try it."

And they were gone, treading back the way they came. When they were far enough away, Damian let his hand slip from her mouth, but he still held to her, keeping her from falling. A moment or so of dead silence passed, Damian listening for the return of Hayden and Blaise, and Serene too fearful to say anything. Finally, the agonizing silence was broken when Damian leapt from the tree, landing softly and setting Serene on her feet.

"What do we do?" She looked up at him with a questioning gaze.

"We keep moving."

Trudging through the underbrush of the forest was nerve-wracking. Every step caused a cracking of twigs and leaves beneath their feet. Though she tried to be weightless, Serene's footsteps were anything but silent in the mute surroundings. Damian didn't seem to be having any luck either, curse words piercing the air as a loud 'SNAP' rang out from beneath him.

"Damn sticks," he seethed, as if that would accomplish something.

His skin glowed a bright crimson where they sun had hit him time and time again. It was a sight worse than any sunburn Serene had ever seen. In the books she read, vampires had a speedy recovery rate. So why hadn't Damian's flesh healed by now in the cool shade of the tress, she sun inching its way down, and the moon appearing to replace it?

When the stars finally danced overheard, Damian grew tense, his motions slowing as he strained to listen through the calls off owls.

"They'll search harder now that the sun is down. We have to be careful. If you hear something get down."

Nodding, she stuck close to his side, peering through the obscure darkness for the demons that she knew were out there somewhere.

The night wore on and they kept moving. Her feet ached with pain from the hike, but it was crucial not to complain. Partially because she feared her voice might attract unwanted visitors and partially because there simply wasn't enough time to squander it away complaining.

The moon overhead broke through a clearing in the trees, glaring down on them with a watchful eye. Damian's skin had since healed, returning it to a flawless granite state. Hours ticked past and midnight fell upon them, bringing more than just the call of the wild.

Whispers echoed through the distance and Serene, recalling Damian's instructions, quickly lowered herself to the damp floor. Within a second, Damian's body covered hers as he encased her in his arms.

"What are-"

"Shh. They'll hear you. They can sense your body heat. I have to cover you."

Footsteps came pounding through the darkness, vibrating the moss-covered floor. Hayden and Blaise came into view, emerging from behind two, large oak trees.

"I swear I saw someone over here," Blaise hissed to Hayden, his eyes scanning the area with lightening-fast speed.

Damian slowly, silently rolled deeper into the shadows, away from the two, Serene wrapped in his arms. She worked to slow her breathing, her heart rate, her pulse—anything that might lead them to detecting her. Her muscles tensed as she held herself still in Damian's arms. If they found her she was dead. If they found her everything would come crashing down around her. Her new found world—her new found trust—everything.

"There's no one here," seethed Hayden, distinct irritation laced through his words. "Let's go."

Brush kicked into Serene's face as the pair dashed away, blurs in the moonlight. When Damian was sure they were gone he stood and released Serene, brushing dirt from his clothes.

"They won't be back here tonight. We'll camp out here."

"Camp out? We don't have anything to sleep in. Or on for that matter." Glancing down to the dirt-laden floor of the woods, distaste dominated her expression. The prospect of sleeping on the cold ground with a million species of bugs didn't exactly scream enjoyable.

"We'll manage." With crossed arms, Damian pulled his shirt off over his head and sprawled it out on the ground, motioning to it with his head. "There."

Gazing at the shirt, she felt bad. Why should Damian have to sleep on the mud while she used his shirt as a blanket?

"Are you sure?"

Non-responsive, he sat down beside the shirt, situating himself as he leaned back, lying flat on the ground. Black strands of hair fell across his eyes, but he stared up through the break in the trees, the moon gleaming down softly on his face. He smiled.

"I love the night. I know, cliché for a vampire, but even before I was changed I was a child of the night." His expression was distant, as if he weren't really there, as if his memories had taken him back in time.

Hesitantly, Serene crouched down and adjusted herself atop Damian's shirt, running her fingers over the fabric before lying back and glancing over at him.

Rouge beams of moonlight shimmered across his pale skin, giving him a handsome, ghostly tone. Her eyes trailed down his body. His muscles ripped down his chest in the moonlight, his abs a sculpture of perfection. Arms so strong they could crush a human skull with ease rested calmly at his sides.

When she looked back up, she found herself being stared down by two intensely violet eyes peering out between wisps of black hair. It was then that she realized she was staring back, finding his face somehow disturbed.

"Sorry, I-"

"No. It's fine." Prying his eyes from hers, Damian sat up, ruffling his hair in frustration.

Having had enough of his cryptic behavior, Serene mirrored his actions and sat up.

"What, Damian? What have I done that is so repulsive to you?" Her green eyes shone brightly with sadness and curiosity.

Swiftly, he shook his hair back into his eyes, disappearing behind his veil, the corners of his mouth turning down into a scowl.

"Nothing! Dammit Serene! Nothing!"

Rage boiled beneath her skin, her blood pumping viciously through her veins. Her heart raced wildly within her chest and she stood, glowering down at him as his eyes rose to meet hers.

"Screw you, Damian! I'm leaving."

Rounding, she stomped through the clearing and disappeared into the shadows of the trees, darkness seeping around her. A rush of wind blew past her face, her hair whirling madly about her. Glancing over her shoulder, she found nothing. Turning back to the darkness, she found Damian staring down with a scorning gaze. The ground fell out from beneath her and she coughed as her body slammed against a tree, Damian's hands pinning her arms.

"You don't understand, Serene. You don't!" His voice was arctic and he pressed her hands firmly to the jagged bark of the tree.

Gnashing her teeth in pain, Serene held her glare, unwilling to back down.

"So help me understand." Her words were practically a whisper.

A range of emotions played across Damian's face, coming and going so quickly that she was baffled. Cocking his head, his eyes were fully revealed as his hair side swept across his forehead. His gaze was magnificent, violet and deep, dancing with hidden pain.

Her stomach knotted, but it wasn't magic. The feeling she had felt under Blaise's spell didn't hold a candle to the unexplainable sensation flooding her body as Damian's hands tightened around her wrists.

There was a moment of hesitation in which his eyes overwhelmed her with the pain he was radiating, and their lips met, Damian applying pressure to her wrists in the heat of the moment. The bark on the tree broke her skin, leaving small pin points of blood along her tan flesh. The scent of blood clouded the air and Damian immediately backed away, his breathing stopping abruptly.

Realizing what had happened, Serene froze. Opening her mouth to say something, she was silenced as he advanced on her, grabbing her wrists forcefully and holding them firmly. Bringing one of her wrists to his lips, he paused, closing his eyes and breathing in deeply, control overpowering all other senses. His lips met her wrist and his tongue danced across her torn skin. The taste was bittersweet to him, and he quickly moved to the next wrist. Violet eyes lowered to Serene who stood rooted to the spot with fear and lust.

With a flash, he was gone, retreating to the clearance, leaving Serene in the darkness of the woods, trembling.

CHAPTER 16

Slowly following the trail of bent sticks Damian had left in his wake, Serene padded quietly through the woods toward their camp site. The trees formed a cracked wall around her, sounds of the night echoing in the distance. Shivers ran up her spine as the haunted calls of wolves met her ears. Perhaps vampires weren't the only fictional characters that had decided to make reality their own.

Pushing the last of the branches aside, she emerged into the clearing. Damian sat in the center, cradling his head in his hands. Approaching him was a gamble. Damian was short tempered and entirely unpredictable at times. Disturbing him in such a vulnerable state was a potential death wish.

Moving with stealth, she assumed he was unaware of her presence. His sudden comment proved her wrong.

"I'm sorry." Two words that seemed to begin each of their conversation. However, Serene couldn't conclude exactly what he was sorry for. For frightening her? For hurting her?

"Sorry?"

"I'm sorry—I'm sorry that I seem so appalled by you," he muttered darkly, keeping his gaze locked on the dirt floor of the woods between his feet.

He had a point. It was perplexing, if not frustrating, to feel him opening up and then suddenly get the cold shoulder and a grimace from him that caused her mind to spin. There was more to Damian than he let on. So many things went unsaid and unheard that his life was one big mystery; a web of lies and self-denial.

Damian's shirt still provided a clean surface for Serene to perch upon. Sitting, she evaded her eyes from him, frantically struggling for something to say that sounded adequate.

"Connecting to people is difficult for me. Especially you," whispered Damian. Every word masked the true picture, the truth behind Damian and his past.

"Why?" came Serene, hesitating.

Damian took a deep, cleansing breath before glancing up to the night sky, stars reflecting off his eyes, spelling out the wonders of the universe.

"Blaise sired me. I assume you already knew that." He paused before going on.

"If done correctly, it only takes twenty-four hours to turn fully vampiric. He turned me and left. Disappeared. I was left alone in an alley miles from my house to suffer the effects of the change. When I awoke, a vampire, I didn't know what to do. I thought that maybe I could simply live life as I had been, but I was wrong. I returned home, in denial about the state of things."

Staring intently, Serene watched as Damian spoke, his eyes never leaving the starry sky.

"Returning home led to the bloodshed of my entire family at my hands. They couldn't stop me. There wasn't time, though my father knew how. He had prepared me for such an occurrence as a young boy. My family was very much aware that vampires were more than fairy tale creatures."

"He taught me that the only way of killing a vampire is by stabbing them through the heart with a dagger designed specifically for such a task. Hollywood made up the wooden stake theory. Anyway, I left the scene, appalled at what I had become. Desperate, I sought out Blaise. I found him, Hayden and Alaria in a small house on the outskirts of town. I've lived with them ever since. Being the youngest, I've followed their orders for decades."

His head suddenly snapped down, his eyes locking with Serene's.

"I never hated you Serene. I'm not like Blaise and the others. We were supposed to make you trust us and in the end I was supposed to-" he broke up.

"I was supposed to kill you. Those were the orders. We were to wait for the call and when it came I was supposed to kill you. I wasn't sure when the call would come. A month after you arrived, two months. I wasn't sure. I don't know why they picked me. I suspect it's because I'm the youngest; a sort of initiation."

"I could sense myself growing a fondness for you. I thought that if I distanced myself from you then it would make my job easier. But I can't kill you, Serene."

Damian was Serene's destined murderer. It all made perfect sense. He was following an order from Hayden. Killing her was his goal, but he had failed, and now he had betrayed his coven in hopes of sparing her life. It was an age old tale. People throughout history had thought along the same lines; that if they could only separate themselves from those they loved then their inevitable death wouldn't pain them. It was a nice concept, but far different from the truth of reality.

Silence fell between them like a brick wall, setting both of them in their own worlds. It wasn't until Serene shifted closer that Damian noted her presence.

"Don't." A warning. A threat. Whatever it was, Serene didn't listen. Inching closer, the warm scent of her skin itched at his nose, the sweet taste of her blood lingering in his mouth.

"Serene I—"

The moment overwhelmed them both as Damian turned. With a moment of hesitation Damian moved, pressing Serene to the ground as he hovered over her. Pinned at the shoulders, she stared up at him, her eyes ablaze with horror and lust as a thousand thoughts fought to overtake her.

He brought his face closer, his eyes boring into hers, willing her to trust him, to accept him—to love him. His aura was calm, yet she knew he was battling an inner turmoil. Hovering over her for the longest time, Serene fought the urge to speak, to assure him that everything would be alright. Finally, when she could bear it no longer, she brought her head from the ground, pressing her lips forcefully against his.

His mouth took hers captive, passion flowing between the two. At once her shoulder was freed from the ground, his hand rushing up her neck and behind her head, holding her head steady against his, their lips never parting. Forgetting that Serene, being human, needed to breathe, Damian pressed on until she broke away, gasping for breath.

Letting up on her other shoulder, he ran his finger tips slowly over her warm skin, his icy fingers leaving a trail of goose bumps in their wake. Serene was so delicate beneath him. So human. So real. So much like those he had hunted in the past. Those he had killed without mercy simply because that had been what he was taught.

Blaise never taught him compassion for humans. Blaise never taught him the beauty of life. All he knew was the shadow of death that consumed his present and future. Part of Damian was certain that the only reason Blaise ever sired him was so he wouldn't have to bear the burden of immortality alone as the youngest. Simply bringing Damian into the life he knew was enough to up his ranking in the hierarchy of vampirism.

Damian's lips dipped to the hallow of Serene's throat and trailed slowly up, following her jaw line, leaving a trail of warm kisses to the base of her ear. Tentatively, she set a hand against his chest, pushing him up off her for just a moment as her gaze searched his for comfort, reassurance, but most of all—for answers. Answers to why this was happening. Answers to if they would survive this—if they'd make it out of this journey alive and together. Serene had never felt this way for Ben. Nor Blaise. Damian sparked a passion within her so furious it would light a million candles over and still blaze on within her. It would power all of the stars in the night sky for years to come and never die. It frightened her. This passion. It had come on so quickly, without warning. Though part of Serene felt as if she had known it all along. As though she had always known, from the very beginning, that she would find such passion when she met the gaze of Damian.

Her hand rose to his face, gently brushing his hair away from his eyes, revealing the intense, violet gaze that stared down at her, perplexed. His eyes held wonder, amazement, and fear. There was power within Serene. He could feel it, but he needed her to feel it. He needed her trust.

There was only one way to survive this. A silent communication began between them through mute stares and expressions. Pain. Understanding. Trust. Moments passed as the pair searched the eyes that stared back at them, neither looking away, both lost in an amazed trance. A fixed notion had filled their hearts and minds and not even God himself could prevent the bond being formed. A mortal and a vampire. Enemies by nature joined by a passion that neither could deny.

His flesh against hers was an unearthly sensation. His lips met hers once again and a cold chill bit at Serene's lips; so cold that it burned. Despite the sudden flare of discomfort, she pressed on, her hands resting on his shoulders, her fingertips pressing against his skin. The muscles in Damian's back flexed as he pressed down on her, a dire need for her touch overwhelming him.

Somewhere in the hour that followed, a hidden passion was revealed between them, bringing them closer in more ways than one. And, as she knew she would be, Serene was frightened. It wasn't a fear of pain or regret, but a fear of what was to come. The stars still shown down on them like tiny miracles in the making and the moon didn't come plummeting out of the sky. Though there were no immediate changes or tragic events, Serene had a feeling.

Her new bond with Damian would be the death of her.

CHAPTER 17

After being curled up to Damian all night, his absence startled her as she awoke. Her skin was cold, masked in the shade just inches from the rays of sun streaming down into the clearing like search lights from the heavens. Damian must have moved them both at some point in the night. Sitting up, her eyes combed the trees until she found what she was looking for; two violet eyes, peering out at her. His hand extended briefly, beckoning her to the comfort of the darker shadows. As she neared, he backed further into the darkness of the trees.

Serene's body ached and her chest seemed to burn from within.

The sudden shade of the woods sent a shock of coolness down her bare back and she shivered, her body calling out in protest. Though the moment his arms coiled around her, pulling her against his chest, she forgot all about her chills and pain and melted into the security of his grasp.

"You might need these." Backing up, he held her clothing out to her, smiling as an embarrassed grin came over her.

Changing in the woods, Serene found, gave her more privacy than back at the house. There were numerous large oak trees to pick from, providing a nice little nook; a sort of make-shift dressing room.

With her body clothed and her hair somewhat smoothed down with a quick run through of her fingers, she headed back toward Damian. She found him soon enough and blushed as he was just slipping into his boxers.

"Sorry. I'll—"

"Don't worry about it," he assured her, smirking a playful grin while climbing into the remainder of his clothes.

With both of them sufficiently dressed, a silence came over them. Damian reached out and grasped her hand, entwining his fingers with hers as he pulled her through the maze of trees, heading further from where they had begun.

After what seemed like ages, Serene's curiosity got the better of her. "Where are we going?"

"We need weapons."

"And you just happen to have weapons buried in the woods?"

He glanced down at her with a bemused expression. "Not quite."

A small cottage came into view, barely noticeable in the camouflage of the woods. Vines crept up its sides, threatening to drag it down. It was an ageless battle between nature and man. Man built up the world and nature tore it down.

Approaching the house, Damian paused, his eyes deep with memories of long ago reclaiming him.

"Is this—?"

"My house."

His childhood house. The house he had grown in before his life had been taken and reborn as something else; a vampire.

Carefully studying the structure of the building, Serene fathomed how it had once been, so many years ago, before age had marred its stony surface. The walls were red bricks, built around circular windows that looked out into the woods like eyes, always watching, always waiting. A chimney broke through the tree branches. What had once blown smoke rings into the sky now sat cold and lifeless. A large oak tree sprang up beside the house, nearly lost to the younger trees surrounding it. This tree was old and withered, clearly worn by the weather and grime it had lived through. A tire swing hung from it, evidence of the childhood memories that swamped the house.

Damian's eyes seemed transfixed, staring at nothing in particular, but lost to the memories of his previous life. What did he see when he faced his house, a symbol of his past, wondered Serene. Did he think of his family and the times they spent together? Did he think of his mother and father and of how wonderful they had been?

No. Damian, lost in the past, thought of the onslaught. His sister's blood, warm in his mouth. His mother, weeping, cowering in the corner as she cradled her dead daughter, and his father, trying desperately to protect his family, to shield them from the monster that he no longer called his son. He thought of how his father screamed in agony as his only daughter was murdered before his eyes at the unmerciful hands of her brother. The memory never left him. It would haunt him for all eternity.

The side door was unlocked, just as he knew it would be. It was early morning and the sun had yet to rise. Pushing through the door, the scent of blood pulsing through bodies met his nose and numbed his mind. He knew he shouldn't be here. He knew the monster within him was untamed; wild and thirsty, yearning for what it was deprived of.

And then he saw her, standing just outside the kitchen door, staring at him with big, green, innocent eyes. The face of an angel. His sister, Darci.

"What are you doing, big brother?"

Her words were nonsense to his ears. All he could hear was the soft, rhythmic beating of her heart as it pumped blood throughout her body. He had closed the space between them within a second, a blur in time as he appeared before her, glaring down with eyes that radiated a thirst that had never been there before.

Darci trusted Damian. He was her older brother. He had always been there for her, had always taken care of her. When she was sick he tended to her and when she was hurt he mended her. What would cause her to fear Damian? Nothing. But as she stared up into his violet eyes, gleaming with a notion that had never possessed her brother before, she met fear.

A blood curdling shriek filled the small cottage as Darci was swept off her feet, Damian sinking his fangs deep within her flesh, her blood seeping through his mouth. It tasted so good to him. So pure and clean and good that he never wanted it to end. He never wanted to stop feeding.

Footsteps thundered down the steps and in a matter of seconds Damian's father stood before him, his mother not far behind, and together their eyes fell on the bloodshed. Damian clinging to Darci, limp in his arms as her blood soaked his teeth.

His father let out a horrified yell.

Immediately, Damian dropped his sister's vacant body to the floor, a new prey set before him. Human reaction took hold and Damian's father ran at him, arms flailing in a barrage of strikes aimed for the creature that had claimed his son's figure. Damian met his father head on, pushing him across the kitchen, knocking over the table, scattering things about. Behind him, his mother scooped up Darci and crawled to the corner, crying over her daughters dead body as she sung her a soft lullaby, easing her tormented spirit.

His father fought with all of the power in his heart and managed to leave a few marks across Damian's face, but not enough damage to stop him.

In moments, Damian's father's body was limp on the floor, blood pouring from wounds all across his body, and blood trailing down Damian's lips as his eyes narrowed in on his last target.

His mother. So delicate and fragile. She'd loved him as a child and had taken care of him as he grew. There wasn't a better mother in all the world nor one that could cook as she did. She was an angel. But not even the mighty were spared and the angel fell like her husband and daughter before her.

And there stood Damian amongst it all, the blood of his family stained in his skin.

The vacancy in Damian's eyes was unnerving and Serene had to shake him from his stupor, a gentle nudge of the elbow.

"Damian?"

"What? Oh." He shook his hair inconspicuously to shroud his eyes. "Sorry."

The house looked safe enough from the distance, but actually accessing it was a different story. Over the years, roots and vines had laced together along the path creating an intricate maze of nature that slowed their progress. Serene tripped more than a dozen times and, though Damian didn't trip, he moved slowly and cautiously, taking twice the amount of time to reach the house than it would have taken if it weren't for the mangled vines.

The door, still standing, was eroded and the doorknob had rusted. Shouldering the door open, a dust cloud rose to meet Damian as he bounded into the room. His breathing stopped as the air filtered out the open door. When the room had cleared, his lungs refilled and he motioned Serene in.

Stepping into the musty house and out of the fresh air, she observed the room she now stood in. Quaint and tiny, filled with odds and ends unrecognizable beneath their layer of dust, the room looked as if it had been crafted centuries ago and left abandoned since. As if the last residents in the house had been Damian's family.

"Stay here. Don't look around," Damian commanded.

He bounded up the stairs and out of sight. For a moment, Serene obeyed and rocked back and forth on the balls of her feet, but curiosity took hold and she moved from her spot, shifting throughout the room.

A handcrafted rug was sprawled out across the floor, a small, family-sized couch to the right. In front of the couch was a table. Running her finger along the surface, a large strip of dust spilled over the edge and disappeared in a puff as it fell to the floor. In its prime, the house must have been quite homey, but now it was cold and vacant—a mere memory of its prior self.

Turning, her eyes met a door across the way. Damian had yet to return and she saw no harm in taking a quick peek.

Treading across the room, her footsteps fell a bit heavier as they left the cushion of the rug. The door stuck slightly as she pushed on it and swung open with a creak. Pots and pans were the first thing that caught her eye. Dishes, an ice box, a sink. The room had all of the accommodations of a kitchen, but it lacked the tidy arrangement the other room had. This room was disturbed, though not recently. The table was overturned and the chairs strewn awkwardly across the floor, each carrying their own shield of dust. And while that was all suspicious, there was a much more disturbing factor.

Blood stains; on the walls, on the floor, on the counters. Remnants of the past. Damian's past. There was no scent, the blood long since dried, but the scene was no less horrific. Her mind immediately questioned whether or not the bones of his family remained. Seeing that they didn't made sense. The bodies had no doubt been discovered and removed soon after the deaths.

"Will you ever listen to me?"

She jumped as his voice shook her and she diverted her gaze from him, finding it difficult to face the monster that she knew he had once been, the monster that had left this mess. Her fingers curled as he took a step toward her.

"It's my past, Serene. I can't escape it and I don't expect you to accept it, but it's my past. I can't change it." His tone was soft, defeated, and Serene looked up to him with forgiving eyes. Before she had a chance to speak he continued, pulling her from the room as he did so and closing the door on the scene and his past.

"These will help us if we are forced to defend ourselves," he explained, catching her perplexed glances to the daggers he grasped. Offering her the smaller of the two, she accepted and ran her finger delicately over the silver blade. Small carvings spelled out words in a language unknown to her along the blade's edge.

"It means 'Faith, Hope, Protection'. My father gave it to me when I was a boy. It's designed for killing vampires. Ironic isn't it?"

The blade itself did not compare to the handle that accompanied it. Pure silver, an emerald inlay that shone as bright as Serene's eyes, and an intricate pattern of carvings encircling the stone. It seemed almost blasphemous to use such an exquisite item for the slaying of creatures. Damian held a dagger of his own with a stunning sapphire inlay and a gold edged blade which he swiftly slid into a sheath he had strapped around his waist. With great ease he reached out to Serene and slid a leather sheath around her waist as well. She set the dagger within it and looked to him for further guidance.

Sliding his hand in and out of his pocket, he withdrew a small vile of green liquid and grasped Serene's hand. Prying her fingers open gently, he set the vile in her palm and closed her fingers around it.

"An herbal remedy. It should help heal you quicker if you're injured, though I don't plan on letting that happen." His voice was guarded as were his eyes and Serene knew it must have been her discovery of his past that was causing his insular behavior.

"Damian, I—" the comforting words planned in her head were cut short as Damian slapped a hand over her mouth. Not out of aggression but out of a sudden fear that flared up in his eyes.

"Shh." He dropped his hand and turned quickly, staring intently at the front door. "Shit. They're here."

"Hayden and Blaise? But how?"

Quickly, Damian spun to face her, an unbridled fear blazing within his eyes that weakened Serene. If he was frightened then how could he expect her to be brave? His fear was out of concern for her, but Damian had prepared her. She was ready.

"Serene, you must run. Go out through the kitchen and out the side door. Run into the woods and hide. Stay there until I come to find you."

"But Damian I can't. I—" A rattling of the door sent a shock of fear through her.

"Dammit, Serene, go! I promise, I will find you."

Forcefully, he turned her and pushed her through the kitchen door, locking his eyes with hers one last time before the door swung shut and a bang rang out as Hayden and Blaise made their entrance.

Without giving it much thought, Serene whirled about and ran through the kitchen, ignoring the blood stains and dodging the askew furniture. She reached the door and pushed hard against it several times until it reluctantly swung open with a groan. It had taken them so long to find the house and gather weapons that the sun was slowly sinking beneath the tree tops, leaving only the cool shadows of the woods to comfort her. Quickly, she took off into the night, a silent tear escaping the corner of her eye.

She knew very well that she might never see Damian again.

CHAPTER 18

Running had never been one of Serene's favorite past times. However, running through the forest with the trees whipping by and the looming fear of the threat she was running from kept her legs moving at an incomprehensible speed. Hardly winded, she kept moving, fear driving her further and further from Hayden and Blaise.

Poor Damian. Tears began to well up in her eyes as Damian's words replayed themselves. *I promise, I will find you.* But what if he couldn't find her? What if Hayden and Blaise killed him and didn't bother to find her? She'd be lost and alone. Or even worse, what if they came after her? Yes, Damian had prepared her with a dagger, but she could never win a battle against them. Not by herself.

The sun had completely retreated for the night, the moon taking its rightful place in the sky. Owls let out low hoots all around her, but their cries were more forlorn than comforting. A twig snapped somewhere behind her and Serene ran faster, tears dripping down her face as she stumbled through the darkness, grasping the tiny green vile, her dagger swinging at her side.

The woods seemed to be closing in around her, the shadows casting eerie figures across the ground as she sped through the brush. Her imagination began to take hold and forms began to grow from the shadows. People. Wolves. Monsters of the night. None of it was really there, but it was all much too real for Serene.

With a sickening sensation, Serene felt something grasp her ankle, sending her face first to the dirt floor ahead. She let out a low groan as twigs ripped against her skin, leaving blood trails in their wake. Dirt clung to her jeans as her knees skidded across the ground. When the ground stopped sliding beneath her, she paused, listening intently for the sounds of footsteps. A moment passed and not a sound was heard. She glanced over her shoulder, expecting to face Hayden or Blaise, but she met dead air. There was no one there. It seemed safe to regain her posture. Pushing herself off the dirt floor, her foot caught again and it was then that she realized the culprit of her fall was a protruding tree root. Laughing weakly at herself, she stood and continue on.

Trees stretched out in all directions, leaving Serene disoriented and lost. Glancing over her shoulder, her mind lingered on Damian and how he was faring against his friends. Immortality wouldn't help him against Hayden and Blaise. They knew how to kill him, being immortal themselves. Her feet began to pound against the ground once more, carrying her far from the duo of death. It occurred to her that she was alone now and there was someone out there who ordered her capture. Who? Who or what would have gone to such lengths simply to contain her and, even more peculiar, keep her alive for so long? If they had killed her sooner it would all be over. More compelling was the reasoning behind their commands.

Snap. The crunching of a twig echoed through the woods, vibrating off the trees leaving Serene to guess which direction it had come from—which direction to run from. Her eyes glared through the thicket of branches surrounding her, two green orbs lost in a field of black. Instincts told her to stop, to hide and wait for Damian, but fear of the unknown pushed her deeper and deeper in the woods, further and further from salvation. Faster, until the world around her was a blur of darkness, a world in which she was caged.

Moonlight broke through the branches as they thinned; a clearing was emerging in the depth of the woods. Perhaps if she could reach the clearing she could wait for Damian there. Pushing herself harder, she moved faster, as fast as her body and mind would allow. With the last ounce of exertion, Serene broke into the clearing, collapsing to the ground as a perception of safety overcame her.

She stood and found herself in a circle of trees, the center entirely cleared out. Shadows stretched out from the edges, leaving the mind to guess at what hid within them. Advancing within the ring, Serene froze as a deep, somber laugh echoed within the trees opposite her. It trailed off, leaving behind an earth shaking silence. Had it been her imagination? She began to think so, but her denial was shattered.

She looked to the shadows in horror as a low, mellow voice called out to her. "It's nice of you to join me, Serene." She couldn't quite make out the face of the man speaking to her. His figure moved smoothly in the shadows of the trees. Blood was steadily seeping from the cuts and scrapes peppering her body as she looked around hurriedly.

Fear crept through her as she came to the realization that she was alone in this. No one was coming to help her—no one. She was going to have to face this alone. But she was ready. Damian had prepared her for this.

Then why was it that as she stood there she found herself shaking; her breathing coming out in deep, raspy puffs.

Serene's mind was racing as she followed his silhouette with her piercing green eyes, never glancing away from the man she knew she had to kill. Everything was weighing on her. It was either his death or her own. Never in a million years would Serene have pictured herself in this situation, about to battle to the death with a man she didn't know. All she knew was that he wanted her dead for reasons she may never understand.

Her hands dropped to her side, searching for the dagger she had been equipped with and her stomach lurched in horror as her hand brushed her flat jeans. Her weapon was gone. Her palms were empty—the herbal remedy was gone as well. In her haste to find salvation she had dropped them in the woods, too rushed to remember to pick them up. She was unarmed and helpless.

Serene soon became aware of the eerie silence slinking across the woods. The only sound audible to her ears was that of her raspy breathing. Suddenly, as if grasping her thoughts, the shadow spoke again.

"I'm sorry that it has to be this way, but you've left me no choice." The man began to advance from the shadows and his face was slowly illuminated by the soft glow of the moon overhead. A chilling, sickening fear spread out through Serene's body as her eyes locked with his. How could this be happening? No, this was impossible. It couldn't be. As he advanced closer to her, she stumbled back, her knees shaking horribly.

Luther Valance stalked from the shadows, approaching his daughter.

CHAPTER 19

Luther stood before his daughter, a wicked grin stretched across two shocking fangs. His skin was as white as the moonlight that glistened against it and his eyes were a deep red, crimson like blood. Dark circles ringed his eyes. He was unlike any vampire she had ever seen; darker somehow.

"My daughter, my daughter. How unfortunate this meeting is, the first in years—and the last." His voice had taken on an ancient tone, infected by the blood of a being that had existed for centuries before him.

This was not the man Serene had known as a child. He was thinner, built, and age had escaped him, leaving him in his former thirty-two year old body despite the forty-five years he had existed. How could a vampire so young, a fledgling, radiate such dark power?

Words formed in Serene's mind, but could not escape her mouth, leaving Luther to continue on, smirking at her puzzled stare.

"I'm sure you are wondering how I have become this—this monster." His fangs lengthened as he spoke.

"Please, Luther, allow me." A voice like velvet hissed out from the shadows. Slender and tall, her black hair falling in waves down her shoulders, Alaria emerged from the darkness, her silver eyes candescent against her porcelain skin.

Serene backed away, fear crippling her.

"Come now Serene, show some respect for your father—your King."

"I don't understand. This—" Nothing made sense. Luther was meant to be dead. Yet here he stood, very much undead as it was.

"Surely you would have figured it out by now, Serene. Hayden is, or was, King of the Coven. And I his Queen. Hayden is dead now, as is Blaise thanks to Damian. I always knew he would turn on us, though Hayden refused to believe and Blaise who simply refused to mark his fledgling as a traitor." She stepped toward Serene, her movements like fire, wild and dancing. "I, however, counted on it and knew that I would need a new mate, a new king."

Backing further from the pair, Serene kept her eyes on Alaria, while watching for movement from Luther out of the corner of her eye.

"Thirteen years ago I met your father in an alley, very much drunk and very much alone. Though even in such a state, I could see the power within him, the undying thirst for life, a thirst that your foolish mother tried to extinguish. It occurred to me then what a great king such a powerful man would make and I took him as my own, siring him and strengthening him with three times the power of any average vampire. I knew that some day we would have to destroy his mortal family."

With a blur, Luther was beside Alaria, grinning.

"Oh Serene, how foolish your mother was. She knew, of course. How could she not? When she saw what I had become she was fearful, more for your life than her own. I lived by night while she existed by day. The neighbors began to postulate, accusing me of cheating. Your mother, being the image of perfection that she had always been, could not have her little world tarnished. She had to prevent any further gossip about the Valance family. Divorce seemed to be the only logical answer. Once I was gone, she built the scene around herself. Poor Silvia, alone and unwanted while her husband was off in England living a life of scandal. Funny how humans eat that nonsense up."

"You continued to reach out to me, however, and I knew that, in time, you'd come looking for me even if I denied seeing you. I knew that I would have to kill you and your mother soon to prevent all of this. I never wanted you to know about the world in which I live, but it's too late now."

"Your mother was creative and faked my death. A plane crash? I was shocked. How unimaginative. It was for your own good, of course. If you believed me dead you wouldn't have come looking for me, or so she thought, and your life would be spared, for a little while anyway. How ironic things turned out, isn't it? My "death" brought on the exact situation your mother was attempting to shield you from."

Tears burned into Serene's retinas as the truth sunk in. Her entire life had been a lie. Her mother had made her father into some lying monster rather than the monster he really was. And for years she had hidden the truth, inevitably faking his death. She had known all along and left Serene to drown in her tears, tears shed for a plane crash that never occurred. And now her father was King of the Vampires, partnered with walking death, Alaria? A world that had once seemed so large was beginning to seem so small.

"I knew you, Serene. I knew you couldn't stay there in that small town much longer. The desire for freedom is in your blood. Blaise had been watching you for a week. When he reported Silvia had faked my death I knew I would have to kill you both soon. Blaise located you on the plane, called me, and I set to work on cleaning up the leftovers."

"Your mother was an easy kill, though I had wished for more of a chase. As far as the town is concerned, she moved to England to live with you. Your friends were devastated, but thought nothing of it besides what the facts presented."

The ground began to spin. Everything was coming to an end. She would die here, alone in the woods at the hands of her father and Alaria and no one would ever miss her. No one would know she was gone. No one would hear her screams.

"Now all that is left of the loose ends is you," he hissed maliciously.

"But why? Why do I have to die?"

"You know far too much to let you live and I'd already planned on killing you as it was. I didn't know it would be this soon, however. The world of vampires has remained hidden for centuries and, though I am very new to the coven, I refuse to see all of their hard work collapse because of one, small, meager teenaged girl. I also refuse to allow mortals to survive under my name. You are the last of this mess."

Pacing backwards, she pleaded with him. "I won't tell anyone. Just let me go, please."

Go where? She had nowhere to go. Her mother was dead. Her friends assumed her gone. Where was she to go?

"I'm sorry Serene, but I can't do that."

With speed and precision, Luther shifted, unsheathing a dagger and sending it speeding straight into Serene's chest, cold hostility radiating from his eyes.

CHAPTER 20

She didn't scream, but fell silently to the ground, blood instantly pouring out from around the wound. The blade of the dagger had dug into her chest and pierced her lung, narrowly missing her heart. Gasping for breath, Serene clutched her chest. The blade was cool as ice against her fingers. Gripping it, she clenched her teeth and yanked, hissing in agony as the blade was ripped through her skin and she lay there, bleeding.

Luther walked to her, looming over his bleeding daughter.

"I'm sorry it had to end this way."

Her eyes met his and slowly, defiantly, she grinned. Fangs sharp as pins grew from her mouth, her lips twisting into a smirk as she brought herself to her feet. Skin instantly grew over where the dagger had burrowed into her skin and she reveled in the looks of shock Alaria and Luther were casting.

His flesh against hers was an unearthly sensation. His lips met hers once again and a cold chill bit at Serene's lips; so cold that it burned. Despite the sudden flare of discomfort, she pressed on, her hands resting on his shoulders, her finger tips pressing against his skin. The muscles in Damian's back flexed as he pressed down on her, a dire need for her touch overwhelming him.

"Damian, you know what we have to do. It's the only way."

Locking his eyes with hers, he nodded solemnly. Immortality was not a gift so much as a curse, a curse he did not wish to burden Serene with, but they both knew her fate if he didn't. She was too human. Too weak. The only way to beat this was to turn her, to strengthen her.

Lowering his head, he buried his face in her flesh where her neck and shoulder met. Breathing in her scent, he closed his eyes, controlling the urge to kill her. Slowly, tentatively, his fangs emerged and he set them against her skin.

She tensed beneath him and he ran a finger slowly down her arm, calming her. Without another moment hesitation, he sunk his fangs into her flesh, her blood gliding over his lips and tongue, trying his hardest not to pull away as she gasped, her nails digging into his back.

When her blood ran thin and her heart slowed, he pulled back and stared down into her nearly lifeless eyes. Quickly, he bit his wrist and watched as blood rose to the surface. Lowering his wrist to her lips, he pressed his flesh to her mouth and watched as she drank, his blood becoming hers. He gave her life after death. He brought her into his world. He made her immortal.

"Good-bye, Luther."

A whizzing sound came from the trees behind Serene and a dagger sped just past her ear, impaling Luther through the heart. His eyes fell to the dagger, the sapphire mirrored in his eyes just before he burst into a cloud of blue flames and was gone.

An ear splitting, banshee-like scream shook the trees as Alaria watched her King die before her eyes.

"You!"

Her eyes were like poison, her movements swift and deadly. Serene watched and backed away, but soon noticed Alaria's gaze was not on her, but directed over her shoulder. Rounding, Serene smiled.

Damian was emerging from the woods, blurring to Serene's side as he picked his dagger off the ground, wiping its blade on the side of his pants.

"Seems I've taken two of your lovers today, Alaria," he mocked, enraging her.

"I always knew I should have killed you. The moment Blaise sired you I knew you were unfaithful."

She danced her way toward him, her skirt twisting with her motions.

"Too late for that, Alaria. Leave before I make of you what I've made of the others—dust."

Damian, who had before seemed reserved, was glowering with rage, protection, and pride. Serene stood beside him, strong and secure in her new form.

"You did this for her!" Her deathly glare everted to Serene. "She has single handedly destroyed what we have spent decades building Damian, and now you have graced her with a life she doesn't deserve? She must die! She *will* die!"

Before Serene could move, Alaria had unsheathed a dagger, words of death inscribed on its blade, and tossed it through the air, straight for Serene's heart.

"No!" Damian hissed and shifted to block the attack.

The dagger dug into his flesh and he hissed in pain. With narrowed eyes, he rounded on Alaria, wrenching the dagger from his arm.

"If a fight's what you want, a fight's what you'll get, Alaria." Damian was quick to return the dagger, sending it hurtling at Alaria who moved swiftly to the side to evade its path. Her smile was cat-like, her eyes slits.

"I don't want to play with you, Damian. It's your little toy there that I'm after." Her eyes flicked to Serene.

Damian ignored Alaria and the two approached each other, moving in circles like two animals about to attack.

Their speed was intense and their motions blurred. Serene followed as best as she could with her underdeveloped powers. Damian struck Alaria with a sharp blow, just missing her heart and piercing her lung. Alaria retaliated with a large gash down Damian's cheek. Though she wanted to help, Serene was rooted to the spot, unsure of what to do.

The power emitting from Damian and Alaria was unparallel to Serene's. Her speed was less and she had never been trained to fight as these two had. All she could do was watch.

The ground shook as Damian charged Alaria. With a flash, he had her pegged against a tree at the edge of the clearing.

"Give up?" he hissed.

"Yes. Let me go," seethed Alaria through clenched teeth.

Released, Alaria limped slightly, glaring. "Why do you care about her so much?" she demanded.

"Because—I love her." Damian looked briefly to Serene.

The next moment seemed to move in slow motion, despite the blurred movements. Damian smiled and Alaria moved. Just as he had glanced at Serene, Alaria struck and Serene could do nothing to stop it.

Alaria flipped around Damian and stabbed, her dagger digging with precision into his heart and, with a swirl of red smoke, Damian was gone, the sapphire of his dagger sparkling in the moonlight as it fell to the ground.

Serene froze. The world began to spin. In a moment she had felt love and lost love and now all she felt was pain. Her eyes swam with tears, blurring her surroundings as she began to choke on agony. Clutching her chest, she stumbled to the ground, her body shaking with sobs held behind clenched teeth.

Damian was dead. Gone. He had died in his effort to save Serene. He had made her immortal to keep her alive. They were going to spend eternity together and now he was gone and Serene was alone.

Alaria was there, watching, grinning, and no doubt waiting to kill. She had to regain her composure. She had to fight.

The salty taste of tears slipped across her lips as tears ran down her face. Through her blurred vision she could see Alaria, grin slipping from her face. Her dance-like poise was changing, becoming more cat-like; defensive.

Alaria's physique appeared unthreatening, but Serene knew better. Beneath Alaria's thin frame was a lithe core, giving graceful movement to her attacks. Her speed alone was double that of Serene's freshly sired powers. Tension filled the clearing, and the air gained a new thickness to it. An unspoken war cry broke out between the two and the sparring began.

Serene was the first to advance with speed like lightening, grabbing Damian's fallen dagger from the ground and slicing through the air. As predicted, Alaria was too fast and Serene missed her by a long shot, whirling around at the edge of the clearing just as Alaria attacked.

First blood was drawn as Alaria lashed out. Nails like talons left a bleeding trail down Serene's arm. This was the first real test of Serene's new form. The smell of blood was strong and tempting, thickening the air around her like a cloud of perfume. The copper scent struck Alaria and a thirsty fire awakened in her eyes and Serene knew she had to attack before it was too late.

With a lunge, she buried the dagger into Alaria, but missed her heart and struck through her shoulder instead. A window shattering screech shook the surrounding trees as Alaria's face contorted in pained rage. But this battle was far from over.

The match continued for twenty minutes, with much stabbing, slashing, slicing and scratching, leaving the moss covered ground stained red with blood from each side. Both girls were trembling with anger and fatigue, despite the unnatural stamina each possessed. For a fledgling, Serene had held her own against Alaria.

Blood was flowing freely from open wounds on both opponents. Alaria moved with pained expressions and Serene's arm throbbed painfully. She suspected it was broken.

"Let's end this now, Alaria." Serene's voice shook with bottled rage and distress. Damian's face filled her mind, bringing fresh tears to her eyes with every given chance.

"Aww. You're going to cry," sneered Alaria, taunting Serene as she moved closer. "You're weak. You've always been weak. The only reason you stayed alive this long is because of Damian Carali, your guardian angel. Well who will protect the little girl now? This is reality. Damian isn't coming back and I'm going to finish what he left undone."

Alaria closed the distance between herself and Serene, clutching Serene by the arm and pulling her in close. Serene was meat in the predator's hands.

"Go ahead, Alaria. Kill me. I have nothing left to lose and you have nothing I want. You have no one. My da-Luther is dead. Hayden and Blaise are dead. You're alone."

Alaria stopped and set her narrowed eyes on Serene.

"Stupid girl. Do you honestly believe that I cared an ounce about any of them? Power will always be my confidant. Your father, Hayden, Blaise—they were all mere pawns in my game of success."

Pushing Serene away, Alaria began to drift to the outer edge of the clearing.

"You're the one alone now, Serene."

Alaria was subsiding into the shadows, a wicked grin teasing Serene from across the clearing.

"Living your life alone and unloved is, and will be, your future. Forever."

Her words echoed around Serene as Alaria disappeared, blurring into the woods, cackling as she did so. When the air was still and silent, Serene's screams of anger and mortification awoke the night. She slowly collapsed to her knees, holding the one thing she had left—Damian's dagger. She wanted to cry, but it was as if she were frozen. Her fingers dug into the dirt as she rocked back and forth, slowly trying to hold herself together. Tears burned the corner of her eyes and she had to force them out. She had to release the pain. A pain so unbearable that crying could never ease it. She sat there in the clearing for hours, rocking herself slowly, clutching Damian's dagger until it dug into her blood stained palms and drew new scars into her skin.

"*I love her,*" he had said.

"I love you too." But it was too late and Serene's useless words faded into the night, unheard.

Time escaped the grasps of the nightmare, and the sky began to fade from black to purple to a light shade of pink as the sun threatened to rise and bring forth another day. It seemed unbelievable to Serene that another day could ever exist in this world where nothing made sense anymore. But the sun did rise, and Serene moved into the shadows, a promise of another tomorrow.

Epilogue

Serene spent many decades searching every crack in the Earth for Alaria. After Damian's death she set out to finish what Damian had begun; destroying his makeshift immortal family.

Tracing her steps back to Damian's childhood home, she found only the dusty remnants of Hayden and Blaise. She kept Damian's sapphire dagger with her at all times, determined to use it to kill Alaria.

She never found Alaria.

She never even found a trace of her existence. Not in the alleys of Russia, the mountains of Peru, or the bogs of Scotland.

Serene told herself time and time again that some other lucky vampire had done the deed before she had gotten a chance. She told herself that Alaria was dust, strewn across the grimy floor of an oily city street somewhere.

Serene returned home only once within the years following her experience. Just as her father had said, her mother was gone. Their house has been sold to a young couple who had, judging by their accents which Serene heard through the dinning room window, moved over from England.

Having learned to keep to the shadows, Serene only watched the couple briefly, imagining what her life would have been had she never run away, never met Blaise—never met Damian. Through the open window, Serene watched the couple like a child might watch a dollhouse and a memory stirred within her. The woman seemed vaguely familiar and it wasn't until memories of Damian burned through her mind that she realized where she had seen this woman before. Before, this woman had been a girl, young and in love with the very man who sat sipping coffee at the dinning room table. It was the couple from the picture Serene had stolen many years ago in the backroom of the bookshop. The very bookshop which began the unraveling of Hayden's plans. Everything had come full circle in Serene's once tiny world. She had saved a life which would now continue in her place.

Her friends had grown and matured without her. While they formed families and had children, Serene remained in her former seventeen year old body.

Ben had moved on, marrying a girl Serene recalled from highschool, though she couldn't fit a name to her face. Marissa and Hailey's friendship fell apart when Serene left, but they too had moved on and molded themselves comfortably into new lives.

Serene had been trying to escape the grasps of her past life when she left and only now did she realize that she had nothing to escape. No one had been holding her hostage. No one came chasing after. No one put their life on hold for her. The world within Covington had entirely faded over the absence of Serene Valance.

She would live alone forever, trapped in foreign world, knowing that the one she had come from had forgotten all about her.

Serene had spent years ignoring her past, denying her identity, and flinching away from love. In the end, Damian had left behind his haunting past once and for all, sacrificing his life for Serene's. Serene's story didn't have as sweet an ending. Confessing her love for Damian had come too late and she found herself alone, irrevocably damned in a world where she didn't belong.

978-0-595-50781-
0-595-50781-6

Printed in the United States
110430LV00001B/83/P

9 780595 507818